The First

Man to Mars

Jon-Jon Jones

To Derek

Probably the world's latest

delivery but I hope you enjoy!

Copyright Notice

The First Man to Mars

How about a Free Book?

Are you ready for your adventure to get even bigger?
If you join my mailing list you will receive a **FREE** copy of
Victorian Adventure Stories plus a bonus short story
that is exclusive to my mailing list subscribers.

To get your FREE book visit

www.Jon-Jon.co.uk

Contents

I The Event

It glistened as it travelled an unfathomable amount of times faster than man could ever dream of. Its course was certain and it surrounded itself with an almighty glowing dress that would have untold stargazers marveling at its wondrous beauty. Across the tenantless realms of space it hurtled, seeking out new civilisations and worlds. As scientists scramble to their microscopes looking for the latest bacilli so there are those whose beady eyes look to the heavens for answers to questions that they do not know.

On that clear summer night there was one such astronomer at the door of his telescope, his single eye searching for something hitherto unknown. At first, he was not sure what he was seeing, just that it was moving, a falling star? He tracked it and was astonished to realise that it was getting closer. Slow like infirmity creeping on the unexpected was the realisation that this was no passing object, rather a comet, and it was on its way to Earth.

How the professor wished that he could see it land. Given the infinitesimal chance that it survived its war with the Earth's atmosphere the possibility was still remote. It could land anywhere and further to that may become no larger than that of a stone in your garden. The summer was particularly good that year and the professor found himself monitoring its progress every night. Out in the countryside the sky was clear and transparent unlike the visual addendum of smog and light that adorns the nations towns and cities. Steadying his trembling hand, he put his hip flask in his pocket and watched mesmerised as the comet became more personable to be with.

It was on the fourth night that he was convinced beyond all scientific doubt that it would reach Earth but where he could not predict. He had been reading up on the sky in feverish temperament in case the years of alcohol had erased his mind's canvas. The professor was relieved to discover that it had not, such was the interest that when he needed to concentrate he could recall what he desired to and yet the more he studied the less he drank. In the daytime he drew calculations and graphs trying to plot its course but there were too many variables for even the best of scientific formulas.

Professor Oakley was dismayed to read in the papers that others had spotted it too and as much as it disgruntled him, he knew he could do nothing but wait. He continued to work on the comet's trajectory and finally made a breakthrough, the professor assumed the drink had taken its toll for it appeared to be heading straight towards him. 'This must be your own fancy.' he muttered to himself throwing another empty beer bottle into the bin.

The professor started sleeping during the day so he could stay up all night in the field behind his house. He positioned himself in a little divot of land in order to avoid unwanted attention.

As the nights and weeks passed the comet grew in size as it approached until it was visible with the naked eye. Professor Oakley was too scared to sleep lest he should miss it landing. Forced by fatigue the meteorite plagued his dreams, he frequently found himself dancing on it and riding through space screaming with joy. Fortune was on his side as when it finally arrived it was indeed night. He dropped his gin bottle as he looked up to see the ball of fire and ice hurtling towards him. The professor ran and dived for cover as he realised that he had underestimated the amount of exponential energy that was about to be released.

In the final minutes of its approach the professor watched the missile shatter and diminish. One large section remained accompanied by a flurry of splintered chunks some of which vaporised in its own wake. Explosions roared all around him, the professor was thrown through the air by the blast, he landed on the grass and as another one hit, he felt the Earth itself vibrate and shudder.

Professor Oakley got to his feet and did not even think to brush himself down despite dirt being all over him and his grey hair was matted with small clumps. His ears were ringing but he ignored it, he ran to the first crater and saw a radiant green rock within. There were several small fires in the dry grass and he rushed to put them out for fear of drawing attention. The professor could not see anyone coming to investigate. His house was isolated by quite a distance but the landings would have been seen for miles around. Panicking he ran to the other fires and put them out, it did not occur to him that he narrowly avoided a brush fire that could have consumed his house.

He needed to carry the rocks inside but how could he do it? They were still smouldering and letting off steam and gasses. The professor realised how unprepared for the event he really was. He was ill equipped to move or even handle the rocks.

The professor ran back to the house and noticed all his back windows were smashed, he did not have time to worry about it and ran into his house to grab blankets then he went to his workshop and collected some gloves, on the way out he spotted his wheel barrow 'confounded fool' he muttered to himself collecting it and putting the blankets inside.

Professor Oakley went over to the crater and threw a thick blanket over the rock, it was large, about the size of a large portmanteau, wearing his gloves he picked it up half expecting to be dead from poisonous gas or from the searing heat but no such thing occurred and he nearly put his back out lifting it. The meteor was so light he jolted himself upright and nearly fell backwards. He placed it in the barrow with the rock glowing bright green like a green beacon to be set in a lighthouse. The professor covered the rocks over with blankets and with the fires extinguished there would be no way for anyone to see that there was anything of interest in the fields until daylight.

In the barn he removed the chunks of comet and covered them all with tarpaulin so if anyone looked in they would not be attracted by a strange green light. He heard voices coming down the country lane. Professor Oakley ran to his house, looked into the mirror and saw the dirt all over him. He ripped off his lab coat, washed his face quickly and tried to shake the mud from his hair. He raced into the parlour and noticed that the front of his house was undamaged and all the windows were still in place, he grabbed a bottle of gin, pulled the cork out with his teeth and then raced outside just as the party was approaching his house as they traversed the road that passed it.

'Why hallo there fo ... folks.' said the professor stumbling through his gate and nearly falling over.

'Hallo professor you are drunk as usual I see.' said a man in a bowler hat.

'A scientific mind needs a helping hand every now and then you know.'

'Did you see the meteor old chap?' said a man with a walking staff that was as nearly as tall as him.

'Is that what it was? I thought I was drunk I have even been out looking for what caused such a tumultuous disturbance.'

'Did you see it land?' asked a buxom lady in a beige dress.

'It disappeared over there, down the road a couple of miles, I saw the flash of light and felt the tremor so could not have been far, I only turned back because I ran out of gin.'

One of the girls laughed.

'Perhaps you can take us to it?'

'I couldn't find it, it has to be two miles away because I am sure I walked a mile and there must be fires, we will soon see its hue.' Professor Oakley lost his balance but managed to stop himself from falling, he took a huge gulp of his gin. 'Walk on I will follow behind you.'

'Ok Professor.' replied his first interlocutor lifting his bowler hat in salute.

'Cheerio old fellow.' said a younger man.

The professor stood in the road as if in an inebriated stupor and waved them off. He could hear their excited chatter as they walked away.

'We'll probably find him asleep in his garden on the way back.'

'Drunken old fool.' said another.

Professor Oakley smiled for he was always drunk to a degree but he was certainly not out of control on that night. He ran back into the house, threw on his lab coat out of superstitious habit and ran into the field. He went to all the deep craters and filled them in as best he could, he got a garden fork and churned up the soil hiding the surrounding marks until all the scorched grass was hidden from view. The professor decided if anyone asked he would say that he was planting a small orchard. No one wandered through this meadow apart from the occasional dog walker and most of them used the footpaths that circumvented the field.

Professor Oakley walked back to his barn and locked himself in, he took a swig of gin, eyed his glowing green prize and rubbed his hands with glee.

II The Professor and his Niece

'It makes a change for you to offer *me* a chance of adventure.'

'I did not say it was an adventure; merely that I had a letter I wanted to discuss with you.' said Professor James who was sitting in his red leather chair.

'Mmm ...' replied Giles, 'we shall see.'

'Well you have let yourself in as usual, so you can help yourself to a chair, indeed and to a drink.' said Professor James reaching for his bottle of beer.

Giles rolled his eyes, took a bottle of beer out of the sideboard and pulled the cork out with his teeth.

Professor James put his broadsheet on the side and picked up a cream coloured envelope.

'I received it this morning. Do you recall Ian Oakley from my university days? I believe you made his acquaintance once or twice.'

'Professor Oakley? Yes I do. It is not from him is it?'

'Yes.'

'James, throw it in the fire, he is a raving madman, a lunatic and I hear in the community that nowadays a drunkard to boot. He had some crackpot theory about dinosaurs having evolved from birds or being linked to them, such absurdity, he disgraced the name of science, his contemporaries and almost put the university out of business.'

'You exaggerate Giles.' laughed he. 'Oxford University is still in fine standing albeit the rest of what you say it true.

Professor James Bedford and Professor Giles Lincoln looked at each other with eyes wide open.

'How in the bloody hell have we missed that?'

'I do not know, I certainly cannot understand how you did, he is your friend after all?' replied Giles.

'I have not seen or heard from him for many years it just did not cross my mind.'

'We have to tell him.'

'I know Giles. I feel awful, everybody laughed the man out of town, rank and academy but he was onto something and now he is a forlorn recluse riddled with addiction. I stood by while he was ridiculed about his theory on dinosaurs being linked to birds and when we found the proof that he was right, his situation did not even occur to me.'

'Steady on chap you were young and just making a name for yourself. There can hardly be blame for that and like you say you have not made his acquaintance for quite some time.'

'Yes, I realise that Giles but we have seen dinosaurs with our own eyes and it was a bloody giant bird with razor teeth, I have one of its feathers in my study for God's sake. I should not have been so quick to judge, after receiving his letter and mulling it over I decided to revisit his theory with an objective mind and was surprised to discover it contained merit, had I have taken him seriously I would have seen that he was right.

'What shall we do? We have been ordered to keep it quiet.'

'Yes, apparently the Queen had severe misgivings over it.'

'I forgot you are friends with Prince Albert.'

'We get along, not sure that he would call me a friend, more a consultant.'

'He never consults me on anything.'

'You are never here Giles. I will introduce you.'

'Never mind all that.' said Giles scratching his shin with his foot.

'Perhaps we can release the information to the public without revealing our source.'

'How?'

'We can use the feather to create a fossil and get it put out in some journals, you know I just met the new proprietor of *The Monarchist* newspaper, *Meppershall* I think the chap's name is, maybe I can get him to run a story.'

'That could work James. It does bother me that the greatest scientific discovery of this century has to be kept quiet.'

'Exactly. I would have to get approval from the university and I had better speak to Gerald. Speaking of letters …' said Professor James pulling the letter out of the envelope.

Giles pulled out his pipe and began crudely stuffing tobacco in it as if he were shovelling coal into a speeding train.

'Let me light this and then you can read it.'

Professor James lit a cigarette and blew out a puff of smoke as if he were somehow blessing the letter. Upon seeing the furnace of his friend's pipe ignite Professor James proceeded to read.

My Dear Professor James Bedford

How the years have passed us by. I remember you with fondness and eagerly follow the reports of your adventures in the newspaper. I even hear there is talk of a book? Do you remember me with kind memories and thoughts? How I trust so as I think you are the only person left I can confide in.

If nothing other than professional courtesy I would ask you to keep the contents of this letter at the sole discretion of yourself and your immediate party. Do you remember the meteor strike of last year? The newspaper's reported that nothing was ever found and the theory holds that it exploded and evaporated just before impact. This is untrue and furthermore it was a deception engineered by myself. It actually landed in the meadow adjacent to my house.

This gift from the heavens has granted many marvellous discoveries and has culminated in the possibility of the grandest adventure of them all - to leave this Earth. Your reaction to this letter is one I have mused over well into the early hours of many nights. The only assurance I can give you my friend is the guarantee of many new discoveries just upon a visit to my dwelling.

I would remind you of our friendship all those years back and implore you to realise the sincerity of my request. Bring trusted companions if you wish but please be discreet.

In friendship and hope.

Professor Ian Oakley

Postscript: Such is my discovery that I have cut back the drink that so consumed me. Also I have read of your friend and compatriot Professor Giles Lincoln and would very much like to meet him.

'What do you think?'

'Leave this Earth? The drink has hold of him. Unless he describes a suicide pact.'

'At this moment we are not at a juncture to doubt him. We were close companions in my early days, he can be eccentric and was the one to concoct an outlandish theory but he was not a liar. He never once pulled a practical joke or told a lie of consequence and even through the alcohol this letter is too coherent. Ian has no one to confide in and I believe that he has made a discovery of some merit, at least in his view. Besides all that we damn well owe it to him now.'

Professor James blew out the last smoke of his cigarette, stubbed it out in the glass ashtray and looked straight at his friend.

'You really think he has something don't you?' said Giles.

'Yes.'

'Then let us leave but I do not know how one should prepare for outer space.'

'Steady on Giles, I said I believe he has something, not that I accept of all his outlandish theories that go with it.'

Giles grunted and blew horns of smoke through his nostrils.

'And the dinosaurs?'

'We will confide in him when the time is right but let us see what he has to offer, if it is a significant discovery we can use it to right his name and then reveal our support for his controversial theory.'

'Wise decision. We need to tread carefully professor because if the devil drink has got hold of him he may be prone to telling all that will hear.'

'The letter suggests not old man. Let us go down for a few days and take some luggage in case we need to stay longer. I will write to him and tell him to expect us on Monday.'

'Sounds agreeable. Who shall we take?'

'Let us go by ourselves for now.'

There was a creak of wood that came from outside the parlour room door.

'*Penny Bedford! Do you eavesdrop at the door again?*'

'Sorry Uncle James, I could not help it, I overheard as I was passing.'

'You were snooping girl do not lie to me.'

Penny looked at an invisible stain on her orange summer dress, as she stepped back slightly the sunlight caught her blonde flowing hair giving her the appearance of angelic innocence, she was holding her study books in one arm.

'Hello Professor Giles.'

'Hello Penny, how are you? Keeping your uncle on his toes I see.'

'Do not encourage her Giles. Penny, I agreed that you could come and to stay with me upon the condition that you would refrain from unruly behaviour and most important of all be discreet in your conduct which means keeping away from my affairs, yet here you are defying me. Perhaps I should write to your father and inform him that this was a mistake.'

'Please do not do that uncle, you know how well I am doing at my studies, the things that I have learnt from you are beyond measure and I do so love living in the country.'

'Penny you have just listened in on a very important conversation.'

'I have. The truth is I have listened in on many of your conversations and have yet to betray your confidence.' Penny put her free hand on her hip.

Giles guffawed and held up his pipe to her.

'You dare to confess such to me? You are lucky I do not fetch a switch.' replied Professor James.

'Stop being so melodramatic.'

'Stay out of this Giles. Penelope if you cannot keep a confidence what good are you? You will never be let into the inner circle of the scientific community. I am most distraught.'

'I am an adult now Uncle James.'

'You are nineteen. Still a child my dear.'

'I am not and the reason I listened in on your conversations is because I have been waiting for this day. You have admitted what a fantastic study I am and what a great scientist I will make and that's why I want you to take me with you to see your friend.'

'I will do no such thing.' replied he.

'You said that I could join your team one day Uncle James and that day has come. And besides I already know about it now so you might as well let me attend.'

'Penny Bedford you are bright and frightfully spirited my girl. I wonder if she would not make an ideal addition to our party?'

'Giles you have always had a soft spot for her which she will unashamedly use.' said Professor James watching Penny flash an innocent smile.

'Please uncle I am dreadfully sorry for my actions but what do you expect being your niece? I am endlessly quizzed about your adventures by my contemporaries and so desperately want to be a part of them. To me it seems quite unfair that I am not. To then spend all my time being quizzed about them is most taunting and injurious.'

Professor James could not help but laugh.

'You should be an actress Penny. How much I see your mother in you sometimes.'

Professor James looked over at Giles who nodded his head.

'Very well you may attend our preliminary trip but I am not allowing you get into any danger. I have a duty to your father.'

'Oh thank you uncle.' said Penny dropping her books, throwing her arms around him and kissing him on the cheek.

'Penny we have a visitor control yourself. Now go and study before I change my mind.' Penny clutched her books and ran out the room, Professor James heard her footsteps thundering up the stairs.

'You knew she listened at the door didn't you?'

'Yes I did Giles.'

'She will make a fine addition, like you she is very smart and solid in her will.'

'I know that and she also kept her trust I have been feeding her falsehoods from time to time and even arranged for people to quiz her but she has never told a soul. If she wasn't my niece I would not feel as much reluctance but the situations we find ourselves in are often fraught with peril.'

'Let us hope that this one is not fraught with laughter and disappointment.'

Professor James got up and looked out of the window onto the front lawn. The sun was shining and bees were milling about the flowers.

'It won't be. I assure you that my old friend.'

III Madman of the Meadow

The sun shone and the green English countryside rushed by the carriage windows like verdant streaks of a painted heaven.

'Oh, I how love the trains they are such marvelous inventions don't you think?'

'Yes Penny, they are rather splendid.' said Giles.

'One cannot help but wonder what the world would be like in a hundred years time.'

'That Uncle James is an interesting question. At an educated guess I would say mechanics could have taken over, it seems to me that engines will drive everything in one form or another and perhaps even the most mundane of things.'

'Do go on?' said Professor Giles taking a bite out of his ham sandwich.

'Well let's take the humble iron, perhaps there will be minute engines in them one day that will produce vast heat and traverse them along your clothes without need of a hand.'

'A little hasty in your imagination but a very clever insight. I think a lot of what you say is too far-fetched to ever become reality but I suspect engines will become ever more important. Professor James your niece has much merit.'

'Of course she does. She takes after me.' said Professor James snapping shut his broad sheet and smiling at Penny.

It was just after eleven when the train coughed its way in to the village of Linden. They stepped off and went through the station house to the taxis. Professor James was surprised to find that there were only a few dogcarts as the growler had just left. They sat on a bench and enjoyed the warm sun, after about twenty minutes the growler returned and Professor James, Giles and Penny climbed in with their cases. Twenty-five minutes later they were heading down a winding country lane and the tracks of a million wheels over the centuries glistened a golden beige in the sun. They pulled up outside the house that stood alone at the edge of a huge meadow with agricultural fields and a couple of huge oak trees opposite.

'This is it.' said the driver.

'Thank you, kind sir.' Professor James said stepping out and paying him.

'You are aware who resides here aren't you?'

'Yes why.'

'Just wanted to check. He is a crazy professor and a drunk, the town folk call him Professor Madman, apparently he is obsessed with milk now according to the local dairy farmer.'

'Might I suggest that you mind your own business. He is an old friend of mine, eccentric he might be yet a lot of his discoveries have more merit than people realise and I do not like to hear that he is the ridicule of the local community. I am in mind not to pay you sir but I shall in order to keep the honour of my party.'

'Professor James, the man did not mean specific offence, he is just one of the crowd, that is all.'

'*Professor James!* I have read about you. It is a pleasure sir. Apologies I did not know but your friend has conducted many a drunken antic in this area I'm afraid and as a consequence rather soiled his reputation. If you say the man has faculties then so be it, you are the one scientist I would listen to, I shall spread the word that perhaps there is much that we do not know.'

'Please do and I would consider that action to be an apology.' said Professor James putting some coins into the man's hand.

They approached the house and could see no sign of life, the house looked abandoned and books were stacked high in the windows.

'I was rather expecting a welcome.' said Penny.

'I hope he has not forgotten us.' added Professor Giles.

'If he has it is because he is busy working.'

Professor James opened the gate. The creak sounded like the cry of a vixen. He rapped loudly on the front door, there was no answer, Professor James called his friend's name and banged loudly, still no answer.

'Come, we will walk around the back.'

'This better not have been a waste of time James. You vouched for him remember.'

'Do not be so quick to make judgement.' replied he.

As they walked around the back they saw the barn door was ajar.

'*Professor Oakley, Ian are you there, it is Professor James Bedford, hallo, are you about?*'

There was a noise from the barn and they all stopped to wait, the door swung open and a man with grey straggly hair and dark grey stubble appeared out of the barn. His face looked weathered and beaten, if Professor James had not known him he would have guessed him to be ten or fifteen years older than he, yet they were the same age.

'*Professor James*, you came, I knew you would old friend, I knew you would, thank you so much.'

'Professor Oakley it is a pleasure to see you. What have you got yourself into this time?'

'In good time my friend. Look at you, you have hardly aged, your hair is still brown and I see you are sporting huge sideburns, lamb chops I believe they have started to call them these days.'

17

'I have had these for years. You have not changed either?'

'Do not lie to me Jim, I have aged greatly like a fool, succumbed to the horrors of alcohol and embraced the way of despair but I see clearly again and at last I think I can bring to man his greatest discovery.'

Professor Giles cleared his throat.

'Ah yes excuse me, Professor Ian Oakley this is Professor Giles Lincoln and my niece Penny Bedford.'

'Professor Giles I have heard so much about you from the papers, pleased to make your acquaintance.'

'A pleasure and please call me Giles.' said he shaking his interlocutor's hand.

'Absolutely and please call me Ian.'

'Yes, it is just him who we call Professor.'

'Nonsense Giles, you and your theatrics.' replied Professor James kicking a plank of wood out the way.

'No, I concur, you have earned it, I read of your adventure in the Indian Ocean, fascinating. The only thing I do not understand is why you are called Professor James? It is Professor Bedford isn't it?' said he pulling a bottle of beer out of his lab coat pocket and swigging from it.

Giles laughed and Penny smiled.

'That Ian, is his doing.'

'Yes, he had a student from abroad who thought James was his surname and took to calling him Professor James. I think it has a ring to it.' said Giles nudging Penny's arm.

'Confounded parlour games if you ask me.'

'Now come on, it has helped to give you some anonymity when required.'

'I will concede the world not knowing my surname ensures I am not flooded with mail and demands.'

'That settles it then Professor and also you are the lead explorationist so the title suits.'

'Ian, that it is another falsehood I am afraid, it is Giles who gets me into all this bother usually and then touts me as the great leader, I am a man of science that is all and I suspect he thrusts me into the limelight to avoid it himself.'

'Is this true?'

Giles laughed. 'He may have a point.'

'Yes I bloody do Giles.'

'I was thinking I do not recall you seeking glory. Scientific breakthrough notwithstanding of course.'

'The Indian Ocean adventure you mentioned, that was him pleading for me to join, as was the Scottish adventure.'

'The Scottish adventure? I never read about that one.'

Giles and Professor James looked at each other.

'Ian, my friend there is much I have to inform you of but when the time is right.' said Professor James placing his hand on Ian's shoulder.

Ian looked into his friend's eyes and nodded, then he looked at Penny.

'And as for you Penny. Your uncle is a fine man so I expect great things.'

'Thank you Ian, it took some persuading of Uncle James to get me here, I am very excited to meet you. He tells me you are a natural scientist so I look forward to hearing of your exploits.'

Ian smiled and led them inside. The house was a mess with dirty crockery all over the kitchen, stains on the floor, sides and tables, the parlour was not much better with dirty mugs and glasses and periodicals and scientific journals strewn everywhere.

'I must apologise I get so wrapped up in my work that I am not even aware of the mess in which I live until someone visits.'

'Am I right in thinking that you will require us to stay for a few nights at least?'

'Yes, Professor if you could.'

'Am I also correct in that an experiment of science will be conducted around this house and on your land?'

'Yes.'

'I mean you no offence Ian but we must do something about your residence, whatever you seek our help with, we need to be organised and thinking correctly, this mess will not abide, so before we do anything let us get this house in order.'

'Sounds good to me.' said Giles.

'Me too.' said Penny looking around screwing up her face.

Ian took the lead by sorting out his journals and periodicals and putting them into boxes, he also returned many books to their shelves including the ones on the windowsill that Penny had seen from outside. Professor James scrubbed the tables and the floors in the kitchen while Giles washed up, Penny cleaned and swept the parlour and took through any dirty cups, plates and glasses through to the kitchen.

They spent several hours working up a sweat and found that none of them could stop, before long the entire downstairs was clean and inviting. Upstairs they ignored the professor's bedroom which was a great mess. The other rooms were used for storage and therefore just needed tidying and a good dust, they opened the windows and soon had the rooms fresh and fit for purpose. They agreed Penny could have the room to herself whilst her uncle and Giles would share the other bedroom.

Once finished they all congregated in the kitchen. It was only then that they realised the professor had no supplies in apart from alcohol and milk. Professor James and Giles borrowed his two horses and rode back into town, then to a sundry store and filled up their bags with meat, bread, vegetables, fruit, jam, butter, milk, potatoes and red wine. Back at the house they were rather pleased with the clean and fully stocked kitchen.

'I feel like a new man thank you.' said Ian as he handed out bottles of beer.

They all pulled out the corks out with their teeth mimicking Ian and spat them out on the floor.

'I guess a little mess is ok.' said he.

'Let us make dinner and then you can tell us all, along with some wine. It has been so long my friend.' said Professor James.

They sat around the large kitchen with a sumptuous meal of lamb set before them.

'Do you remember the time when it was snowing and we took those large wooden trays from the sideboard in the great dining hall and used them for sledging, Ian?'

'Ha, yes I do Professor James. Only we did not realise they were antique at the time.'

'We certainly did not. We would not have taken them otherwise.'

'They did make awfully good sledges mind.'

'You know I think that the Professor is still hunting us now.'

'By chance you should say that, he was speaking near here not long ago and I caught up with him.'

'What was his name?'

'Professor Wilstead.'

'I know Professor Wilstead he taught me as well.' said Giles cutting one of his potatoes.

'Ah yes, that would be him, how is he?' said Professor James.

'He is starting to look like one of the fossils he lectures about but other than that fine.'

'He always did. He probably just moved from Jurassic to Cretaceous.' said Giles

They all laughed.

'He quizzed me about the two trays and said that he suspected some young lads had thought they might make excellent sledges as there was a lot of snow at the time. He was giving me that look that he did whenever we were late. I think he was on to us.'

'I hope you did not confess to it?' replied Professor James.

'Not at all. I denied it but he knows it was us.

'Next time I make a donation to the university I will tell him; perhaps that way I can avoid the cane.'

Penny burst out laughing. 'Stop making me laugh. I can't eat my dinner Uncle James.'

Professor James noticed that Ian had a serious look on his face.

'What is it old man? You look perturbed?'

'Yes, I was just thinking that.' said Giles.

'I was recalling my encounter with Professor Wilstead. I went as I could not resist the topic of palaeontology, he was pleasant enough to start with but when we moved onto science he ridiculed me, I was trying to avoid the bird theory but he went straight into it, I was drunk which helped and like a fool tried to explain my position. A failure of a man I have become and to some degree I accept it but it riles one when someone you admired treats you so.'

'Well Ian I think you will be vindicated and he will humble himself before you one day.'

'How much wine have you had Professor?'

Giles laughed.

'Do not forget the reason we are here Ian. Do you not have an exciting discovery to show us?'

'Yes, I suppose I do.'

'There we go then a toast to your success.' said Giles lifting his glass.

'And restoration.' added Professor James.

'Here, here.' shouted Penny.

'I have to say Giles you have done an excellent job with the meal.' said Ian. 'Did you train as a cook?'

'Thank you. Not intentionally but if you want to captain a ship it is a vital skill. If the chef dies or disaster strikes it is valuable expertise to be able to cook for your men.'

After dinner Professor Oakley got a bottle of scotch and placed it on the table along with three tumblers.

'As you know I am weaning myself down from the alcohol and so drinking less volume, I partook in the wine tonight but am on beer as a general rule, my hands have stopped shaking now and I am convinced that I am close to completely giving up.'

'That is excellent my old friend, from what I can see it has done you no favours, now tell us why we are here?'

'Do you recall the meteor shower last year?'

'I do. You mentioned in your letter that they did not burn up as described in the newspaper.'

'Confound it I forgot about that. Shouldn't have taken the risk really. Come and look out the window.'

Ian got up and walked to the kitchen window. The evening was coming in but being the month of June it was slow and respectful.

'Can you see the young trees that are planted in clusters sporadically over the field? Well that is another one of my crackpot experiments, apparently if you plant trees in a cluster at a certain distance from each other, they will grow three times as quick. They call me Professor Madman but this madness is utter nonsense that I fabricated to cover the sites where the meteors struck.'

'Ingenious.' remarked Giles.

'I told you.' said Professor James.

'So no one at all suspects that they landed here?' said Penny.

'No, the grass is long, I managed to put the fires out and because it is a wild meadow there was nothing to see from the road once they had been extinguished. It also took people a long time to arrive in search of the fallen star. Once I had the new material in my workshop I experimented in earnest and discovered that it is unknown to man. It is probably stronger than diamond yet possesses qualities that defy description.'

'Such as.'

'In time Professor James. Tonight is just a synopsis. Not only is it extremely durable but under the right conditions it can be flammable and burns with an intensity like nothing else on Earth. The minutest of amounts can burn for weeks; it is indeed a marvel of unequivocal proportions.'

'By Jove you have made a discovery.' cried Giles.

'The story is far from over. Hidden in one of the meteors I made another discovery.'

'You jest, surely?'

'Professor James would I call you all the way here to jest.'

Professor James looked at his interlocutor and felt ever more vindicated for defending his old friend.

Ian opened another bottle of wine and poured himself some.

'What you are not seeing is the combined outcome of all my discoveries. It could be possible to do the unthinkable, to take science and indeed man himself to the highest rung of achievement. To do something no one has ever dreamed of even being imaginable let alone realised. Could we finally achieve the unthinkable and make the greatest discovery in the history of mankind? I have brought you all here to ask you one question and one question alone – will you accompany me to Mars?'

IV Secrets of the Barn

All three of them found themselves unable to speak.

'Blasted mumchancer's the lot of you.' laughed Ian.

'Mars you cannot be serious my old friend?' said James.

'I have done the calculations and there is no reason why it cannot be achieved.'

'We will need something to travel in of course but that is why I called upon your expertise. I require a team of trustworthy folk to even stand a chance but I am convinced we can do this.'

'Ian, I hold you in great esteem as a trusted colleague of my old friend Professor James and I believe we even met a couple of times.'

'I can vaguely recall you, there is something about your voice that is familiar.'

'Forgive me for saying that you are probably mistaken. I have no doubt that you are onto something of great value to the scientific community and perhaps mankind itself but

Mars is too far forward old man. We cannot even get in the sky yet, let alone to Mars and what about the Moon?'

'We can see the moon with telescopes I want to prove to the people that I am no fool. I have been ridiculed ever since I suggested a correlation between dinosaurs and birds.'

'Do not dwell on that now Ian like I said you might be vindicated yet.' said Professor James.

'My theories will hold true, I am sure of it, tomorrow I will show you what I have learned and you will see the possibilities I speak of are factual rather than fanciful. The focus of myself is entirely on Mars at the moment but I believe that meteor was a gift from the heavens to aid me in righting my sullied name. So, let us drink and have fun, then on the morrow I will show you all.'

The guests tried their best to persuade Ian to tell all that night but he held fast and the subject eventually changed to their university days. Ian and Giles found themselves competing for who had had the funniest experience with Professor Wilstead. Penny listened intently and lapped up every story with great excitement. The sun against its better judgement eventually set. The party were all inebriated by now and Professor James pretended to ignore that fact that Penny had matched them on every drink.

The next morning Professor James tore open the curtains with enthusiasm and the sun poured in through the glass forcing him to close his eyes. He opened the windows and breathed in deeply as the fresh air came racing through like a pack of wild horses. He went down for breakfast and found he was the first one up. He lit the stove and made a cup of tea, as he sat down at the table Giles came in and used some of the water to make himself a cup.

'Do you think he really has found a way?'

'I don't know Giles but as I said before he is not to be underestimated, this is not a waste of time that I am certain of.'

'I believe you but Mars is too farfetched for my liking and let us not forget we have discovered remarkable things that mankind had no inclination to even dream of, but Mars? A step too far if you want my opinion.'

'If we had just met and I told you of our adventures, would you believe me even for a second?'

'No, I suppose I wouldn't.'

'There is no suppose, you would not even contemplate me, you would probably go around calling me names like-'

'Professor Madman.' said Ian.

'Sorry Ian we were just discussing your Mars theory.'

'It is quite alright Giles. I would think *you* were the madman if you did not have some doubt.'

Professor James sniggered.

'What is with the milk Ian?' said Giles.

'What do you mean?'

'The cab driver who dropped us off said that he heard you had become obsessed with milk. Is it what you are drinking instead of alcohol all the time?'

'I am still drinking alcohol.' said Ian grabbing a bottle of beer for breakfast. 'That wretched farmer never minds his own you know and every time I see him he has something to say about someone in the town. There is a scientific answer to your question in good time.' said Ian swigging at his bottle heavily and marching to the window with his chin in the air.

Professor James looked at Giles.

'Forgive me Ian, I am still waking up and fancy that came out in the wrong fashion, I did not mean to pry or to sound accusatory in anyway.'

Professor James lit a cigarette and exhaled his first plume. A silence fell among them which he enjoyed as he was used to being alone in the morning and treasured his first smoke of the day. He thought he might venture out into the meadow with a cup of tea next time. The professor could not help but wonder what the day would bring, disaster or fortune, it was true that he fully believed that there was scientific merit to be found here. Yet deep down he was as sceptical as Giles about being able to visit Mars but he could not bear the thought of his friend being ridiculed again. Professor James wondered whether it was the right decision to hold back the truth regarding the dinosaurs. As a scientist himself he concluded that even a welcome distraction was still a distraction.

Penny appeared half an hour later and they sat drinking tea listening to Penny crunch her way through some lard on toast.

'I promised to tell you all today and indeed I shall. Perhaps a tour in chronological order would be best.' said Ian.

'Chronological?'

'Yes Penny, meaning we start with the crash sites.'

'That sounds apt.' said Professor James swilling the last of his tea and lighting a cigarette.

'Let us make hast then as we shall have much work to do.' replied Ian.

The party all looked at each other. Professor James insisted that they cleaned the kitchen thoroughly before leaving off. Giles rolled his eyes and started washing up.

The morning sun basked everything in a reassuring warmth. They heard and felt the wet long grass whipping their legs as they walked.

'Notice how the ploughed area is much larger than the area required for the number of trees. This is because I only had a few trees for each site. It is quite remarkable that no one has pieced it together really.'

'You are the only house for some distance I take it?' said Giles.

'You are correct and thank God as I would never have been able to keep my discoveries a secret. If you look over there you can still see some of the burnt grass.'

Professor James bent down and picked some blades of the burnt grass, he looked at them closely and then held them to his nose.

'Odd.'

'Why is it odd Uncle James?'

'Because Penny you must more than merely observe. The grass is burnt as you can see but it should not be.'

'Why ever not?' said Penny picking a blade for herself.

'Because the meteor crashed a year ago. Why has it not regrown? The rest of the stalk is still healthy yet it has been unable to get past the scorched matter.'

'Indeed Professor James, you are still as smart as you were when we first met, that never even occurred to me.'

'I thought you had hidden all the scorch marks and burnt grass Ian?'

'Yes I have but I could not resist leaving a small patch; posterity I suppose.'

They inspected all the impact sites. Professor James collected samples and labelled them separately, assigning each site a letter of the alphabet. He also took measurements of the impact sites whilst Penny who was an excellent artist made accurate sketches of their outlines. Giles studied the base of the tree and the dirt to see if anything unusual had grown.

They walked slowly back towards the barn where Ian had his workshop. They approached the barn and he unlocked it with a large iron key. Professor James grabbed the warm wood and pulled the door open, there was straw all over the floor and it appeared to be a normal barn. They walked through avoiding many of the hanging implements that hung from old rusty nails and clanged noisily when moved. At the back of the large space was a wooden room with a window and another door that looked like it had not been opened in years. Professor James looked around studiously seeing nothing of interest and wondering whether his friend had cracked up after all. He remembered the sample of grass in his pocket and held his faith.

'There is nothing here Ian. Have you been leading us astray?'

Professor James threw Giles a dirty look.

Ian smiled.

'What are you up to?' said Professor James.

'That wall is a door.' said Penny.

'By Jove she is right.' said Giles.

'I suspect your niece is the smartest one here.' said Ian with a wry smile and pulling a lever hidden behind a milk jug, a large portion of the wall swung open to reveal another room.

'The first thing they saw was a strange green hue that lit them all up.'

'Come on in my friends there is much to show you.' said Ian beckoning with his finger.

The party remained silent as they walked in and saw all the science apparatus upon work benches. There were samples and tiny fragments of green diamonds in various clasps and tubes, they walked around the corner and came to a huge cavern. On the floor down below were huge green glowing rocks, their sparkle was as magnificent as their beauty and the light was more captivating than a roaring fire in the middle of a forest at night.

Professor James looked and felt himself threatening to become emotional, he had trusted his instinct and now truly saw that his old friend was still the genius he had always been. He vowed to himself to set right his friends false record and to restore his reputation in the world of science and indeed in the whole country.

He walked around looking at the strange experiments and finally he walked down the steps into the cavern realising that he was now underground, he approached the largest of the green glowing rocks and reckoned it to be the size of a pony. It had vapour coming from it, he put his hand through it expecting to be scalded by either heat or ice but there was nothing, he leant into smell it but it was odourless. Professor James heard Penny coming down the stairs after him and motioned her to stay where she was.

He walked around it inspecting it closely, he pulled out a magnifying glass and examined it, the meteor seemed to consist of super high-quality glass or diamond. Putting his magnifying glass away he stretched out his hand to finally touch it. He looked at Ian who was now standing behind him. Ian gestured for him to go ahead.

Professor James put both hands on the comet, it felt as smooth as glass which was bizarre as the ridges were almost indistinguishable by touch, it had no temperature like putting your hand on the wall of your parlour.

'Remarkable Ian, truly remarkable, what have you learnt about it?'

'Come back upstairs and I will show you.'

They followed and went back upstairs, Penny ran down and quickly touched the large meteorite before joining them. Giles scolded her advising that there was plenty of time for that later on.

'Professor, you see that nugget on the bench? Hit it as hard as you can with that hammer.'

'Professor James picked up the lump hammer measuring the weight of it with his hand.

'This is a heavy hammer Ian; are you sure?'

'Trust me, hit it and as hard you can, do your damndest to smash the thing into smithereens.'

Professor James waved everyone back and swung the hammer over his shoulder and down on to the wallet sized piece of meteorite as hard as he could. The hammer stopped dead as if he had struck the ground.'

'Inconceivable. There is not even a blemish.'

Giles walked over and examined it. 'What on Earth could it be made of?'

'That is the point it is not from Earth, but there must something that compromises it?' said Penny taking it from Giles hand.

'The strength of it is incredible. Have you managed to break it?' said Professor James.

'Not exactly. But you see its usefulness? It has survived the darkest recesses of space and an impact with Earth. The element is very difficult to ignite, you see that box over there, underneath is a tiny fragment that I managed to ignite a month ago and when I say a tiny fragment, I mean the size of your fingernail.'

'A month ago? It will be extinguished by now old man.' said Giles.

'And no oxygen so the flame will not burn.' added Penny.

Professor James remained silent, he was deep in thought and reflecting on the gravitas of his friend's discovery, he realised it could change everything they knew about minerals and science. The applications were already numerous, this had to be handled carefully, they would have to know exactly what they were dealing with and how the world would react to it. Professor James wondered if there was a way to artificially produce it.

'You might want to prepare your eyes.' said Professor Oakley walking over to the box.

Before anyone could respond Professor Oakley lifted the box and a bright light dazzled them as they if they had just immersed from a cave on bright summers day.

'The blasted thing is a bright as the sun I swear it.' said Giles.

'The ferocity of which it burns.' added Penny.

'Quite.' said Professor James.

'Here are some goggles I have made for you all.' said Ian handing them out.

They put on the crudely made blackened glass goggles, looked at the tiny burning splinter and saw that just one end of it was alight but burning as if a welder had his torch to it.

'That nugget was exactly the same size a month ago, look at the projection of the flame, if that was not securely fastened the energy would send it hurtling around the room, for an immense amount of time.'

'This is how you plan to drive the craft?'

'Exactly Professor James. Look how much we have and there is more to show you still.'

'Craft?' cried Penny.

'Yes Penny, if we are to visit Mars we will need something to travel in.' replied Ian.

'A capsule. We require a capsule.' said Penny.

'Steady, we have only just begun to learn what is possible, we must tread with caution before we make assumptions about what we can do.'

'I assure you Professor James we can go to Mars and we shall go to Mars. You recall we discussed milk earlier on?'

Professors James and Giles nodded.

'Well the truth is gentleman and lady of course.' he said remembering Penny at the last minute. 'That I do have penchant for milk and drink it frequently when I'm able as I found it most disagreeable when drinking alcohol so to avoid vomiting I only drink it in my tea.

When I began to reduce my drink intake I recalled my love for it, treated myself to a bottle and drank the whole bottle there and then. I decided that this could be my treat for giving up alcohol and how apt it proved to be as I could not stomach it after a drinking session so in order to get my reward I would have to ease my alcohol intake.

I appreciate this might seem awfully trivial but when you live alone with nothing but your own wits you will be surprised how the smallest of things can render the highest value. I treasured my milk and found a heightening sense of victory every time I drank it as it was another step forward to being sober. And so I got in the habit of drinking it when I was working, one day I placed a bottle on the worktop as I was conducting my experiments and when I reached over to grab my pliers I accidentally knocked over the bottle of milk. It promptly spilt all over the work surface and all over a nugget of meteorite. Do you want to know what happened?'

'That's a bloody stupid question Ian.' said Professor James before anyone could say anything.

'Let me show you then.' said he pulling out a bottle of milk that had been hitherto obscured by apparatus. He took another nugget of meteorite and placed it on the floor. 'Observe.'

As soon as the milk hit the meteorite it began to writhe as if it was somehow organic, it then started to grow in size and they watched as it doubled its mass again and again. Ian picked up the hammer and brought it down on the growing meteorite, a large chunk fell off.'

'I told you there is always a weakness.' said Penny.

'Look at it, it's still growing, even the part that has been severed.' remarked Giles.

'That is so strange.' said Professor James.

'Bizarre and unprecedented.' said Giles lighting his pipe.

'Quite. What we have here is a true discovery and one that will change the course of mankind and indeed history itself, you are to be congratulated my old friend not just for what you have discovered but for the prudence you have shown by not announcing to all and sundry, like many people would have been tempted to do.'

'If I am understanding you correctly you are saying that we can use this substance to protect the capsule from the harshness of space whilst using it at the same time to propel us through the heavens at an extravagant rate.'

'That is exactly what I am saying Giles.'

Giles looked at Professor James who acknowledged him.

'The theory is starting to hold up.' said Professor James.

'You mean we really can go to Mars?' exclaimed Penny.

'That is not quite what I said. In theory this strange substance does appear to have the qualities to both protect and propel us, if we can learn to control it. I am still not convinced but your idea grows in merit.'

'If it becomes weakened by milk then we have a means of controlling it.' said Giles.

'Yes perhaps.' replied he.

'The thing that I am curious about is what property in the milk is it reacting to? Why milk? Why not water, beer, gin or any of the other numerous liquids on Earth?' said Penny.

'Are we thinking the same thing Ian?'

'I think we are James.'

'Calcium.' they said in unison.

'Before we discuss this any further I think an agreement must be made. We are talking about things unknown to science and man, we must judge and process rationally whether we are going to realise any of this speculation. We cannot mention a word of this to anyone, not even our most trusted of confidants, not your priest, wife or anyone. There is a huge power in this discovery and every nation on Earth would seek to understand and harness it.

From this moment forward this is a top-secret science experiment, let us work together to understand its properties and potential, then test them to the full. When we have its full capabilities we shall be able to make an informed decision. It could even be that it is too dangerous to be discovered, do not forget as scientists we must be responsible and if the responsible thing to do is to remain silent then so be it.

Anyone who wishes to remain in our company swears to complete secrecy and loyalty to the group. We will watch out for each other, ensure that we are fit and well both mentally and physically, nurture each other in spirit and there shall be no mockery of theory or suggestion. Who would have believed me five minutes ago if I told you the key to unlocking this meteorite was milk? Not one of you because we are scientists who are doubting what is possible in the unknown. Anything is possible in the unknown that is why it is the unknown. Do we agree?'

'I completely agree with Professor James let us form a team and work upon its secrets day and night, let us gather all we can. Professor James should lead the team and say what is to be disclosed and take the decision about any exploration voyages.'

'Confound you Giles, why do always want me to be the leader?'

'I agree with you Giles, Professor James should lead this team forward and decide whether it is possible to go to Mars after all.'

'I second that motion.' said Penny wafting Giles' pipe smoke out of her face.

'One thing is for sure Professor Ian Oakley, this is your discovery and if anyone shall be remembered for it, it shall be you.'

'Thank you, my old friend.'

'No, you do not understand as you know I am now a man of considerable influence and perhaps I owe you sincere apologies, deep in my gut it has bothered me for many years that you were laughed out of the community. I was preoccupied with my own adventure and experiments I neglected our friendship and when you needed me, I was not there. I happily watched as you slipped into alcoholism and destitution. Now I see that you always deserved to be recognised and old friend I look you in the eye and proudly announce that you are a better scientist than me, you have done us all proud and you are the example to live up to.'

Ian had tears welling up in his eyes.

'Come my friend, let us not have any of that. You will start young Penny off.'

Penny remained silent.

'Well I have to say what you have discovered is quite remarkable. I hope you do not mind me making an observation.'

'What is that Giles?' said Ian.

'I must warn you it might shatter your hopes.'

Professor James and Penny stared at Giles who ignored the perceived peer pressure to back down.

'Matters not, we are men of science and besides this is a great discovery in itself.' replied Ian.

'That it is but it will be of no use even if we do find a way to get to Mars.'

'And why is that?'

Professor James realised what Giles was going to say and wondered whether he should interrupt, it may be too early to knock the professor off his stool. The once strong and confident man of science, albeit still a genius, was a shadow of his former self, a ghost of the man who he once was. But Professor James was surprised to see a wry smile on the Ian's face. A smile which he had not seen in many years.

'We cannot go to Mars as we will not be able to breathe. It is a grand idea and very inspirational but quite impossible.' said Giles.

'Is it really? Shall we finish the tour.' replied he.

V Manna from Heaven

'What else have you been up to Ian?' said Penny collecting a small rock of meteorite and putting it in her pocket.'

Ian remained silent and led the party back down into the cavern where the large meteorite was. He proceeded past it to a big set of wooden doors that were hidden in the shadows. There was a huge lock on it and Professor James noticed that there was something not quite right, there were rubber seals around the frame and it looked as if the wood was stuck onto the door rather than actually being made of it. His suspicions were confirmed when the huge door clicked open sending a loud noise reverberating around the room like a gunshot in a cave. The doors were thick metal and lead to a huge cavern.

A green light with a strange purple hue gushed out of the room lighting them all up as if they were phantoms of the night, they followed Ian inside and found themselves startled by the huge clang as he brought the giant iron door to a close.

The room was filled with huge plants, all of the same variety, they had giant leaves that were thick and looked like rubber with large pulsating veins as if they were the scales or feathers of some giant creature. Professor James noted that this was a greenhouse but devoid of light, he wondered why and approached one of the plants. He looked at Ian who nodded his approval. Professor James noticed that he was grinning like a man who had just found his fortune.

The plant felt like vulcanised rubber, Professor James squeezed it and could feel how soft and spongy it was, he closed his hand tight but the plant still returned to its original state. He turned the leaf over and saw the purple hue was coming from the underside of the leaf. He decided to rip one off so he could inspect it and perhaps take it back to the house for further inspection. It did not rip, he tried again, perplexed, Professor James, who was a strong man by his own standard, grabbed it with both hands and tried to rip the leaf but could not. He only realised that he was being watched when they all started laughing.

'Remarkable.' said Penny.

'Have you been eating your vegetables?' said Giles.

'Be my guest.' replied Professor James.

Giles walked over and wrestled with it but to no avail.

'Remarkable indeed.' said Ian with a smile.

'May I try?'

'Why of course you can Penny but I fear you will not succeed you can hardly claim to be as strong as your uncle or myself.' said Giles.

Penny smiled and walked over to a work bench that hitherto had not been noticed, Penny picked up a knife and checked it was sharp with her fingers, then walked to leaf and began to slice it, at first nothing happened but then she applied a lot of pressure and using the carving knife more as a saw than a blade she started to get through it, she pulled the leaf off and handed it to her uncle.

'There you go uncle that wasn't so hard was it?'

Ian clapped loudly. 'What a team we will make.'

'Well done Penny. How did you know to use the knife?'

'It was a simple deduction there is nothing in this room except those plants and very sharp knives on that bench, there is only one possible explanation for them being here, especially when you can also see small pieces of plant on the floor next to the work bench.'

'You take after your uncle, Penny. It will be you leading these expeditions one day.' said Giles throwing his arm around her shoulder and pulling her in tight.

'This plant,' said Ian walking over taking a blade out of his pocket and sawing through the stem with remarkable speed, 'has some remarkable properties too as you shall see. Would you believe that all this has come from a tiny bud no bigger than your pocket watch?'

'You jest, surely?'

'No Giles I do not. Once I had hauled the comet fragments into my barn I decided to inspect every inch with a magnifying glass hoping I may spot something buried inside one of them.

As I inspected the large rock, diligently viewing every nook and recess, something drew my attention. I quickly realised that there was something either stuck to or growing from it and I was terrified that I might inadvertently destroy it. The sample was so small that I dared not remove it all from the green glass rock in case it perished right in front of me.

It took me many days to decide but the more I studied it and the more impossible it seemed, the conclusion was forced upon me that this was indeed extra-terrestrial plant matter. With no frame of reference to go on I figured that it had survived the most remarkable conditions to arrive here so it must consist of a very sturdy nature. It was then that I decided I might be able to treat it like a normal plant and figured I could take a sample and plant it, then examine it closely. As you saw taking a sample is no easy feat, I used a pair of secateurs and managed to get a sample cut off with great difficulty. Later on I experimented with knives and found it to be a lot easier.

I planted it in a small pot and then began my examinations, it was then that I caught a shallow purple hue

41

coming off the underside of it. I left it on my bench and carried on with other studies, I was drinking and working away merrily as was the usual occasion but as I finally turned to go to bed, I could have sworn that the plant had already grown. I looked again and realised that I had never measured it in the first place so I took its dimensions and hastily scrawled them down. In hindsight I should have just took it over to the remaining piece still on the rock for comparison.

The morning had me hungover as usual and checking on the plant had slipped my mind. I remember not what I had to do that morning but suffice to say I was running errands and in all likelihood buying more drink. When I arrived in my shed there was no question to whether it had grown or not. It was enormous compared to the night before.

I beamed with excitement at the possibilities of this wonderous plant. Have you not all realised that it survived entering the Earth's atmosphere, I have tested it and it seems unperturbed by fire, I mean it does not even try to avoid it, the plant does not heat, does not burn, the most miraculous plant I have yet to encounter.'

'Anyone has to encounter. What else have you found out about it?'

'That my dear Professor James Bedford you may be able to tell me. Walk through the plants with me. All of you.'

They all followed Ian as he walked through the plants. Some of the leaves were the size of small ponies.

'Tell me, were any of you feeling somewhat lethargic when you entered?'

'I admit the alcohol had its impact yet I have been feeling rather adequate this morning.' said Professor James.

'You can add me to that list.' remarked Professor Giles.

'Well I have to say I have felt wide awake all morning.' said Penny.

'That is truly the voice of youth among us. Tell me how do you all feel now?'

'Why I feel incredible?' said Giles.

'What about you Professor James?'

'Thinking about it I do feel rather good as if I have just been born. Energetic and lithe.'

'Excellent. Penny what is your status?'

'I felt awake but now I feel as though I will never require sleep again.'

'Is it the plants that's making us feel like this Ian?'

'Indeed it is Giles. The plants are pumping out pure oxygen at an incredible rate. There is also something else in the air but I cannot place what it is. Our energy levels are incredible.'

'Much more so than what oxygen alone would provide.' said Professor James putting his face into a plant and inhaling deeply.

'That is not all, it does not just work in here, you will be energised and awake for many hours after leaving.'

'In a way it gives us some kind of power and makes us super.'

'Hardly Penny, I think you are perhaps taking it a step too far.' replied Professor James.

'These plants are powerful enough to provide us with air. Even in airless environments.' said Ian smiling and pulling a bottle of beer out of his pocket then gulping down a large mouthful.

Penny and Giles stared at him with mouths agape.

'In theory if these plants can hold out like you indicate they could be used to breathe in space or on another planet such as Mars.' said Professor James.

They all stood in silence as the realisation occurred to them one by one, they could breathe anywhere, underwater or outer space.

'You really have made quite the discovery Ian.' said Giles.

'Indeed you have.' said Professor James placing his hand on Ian's shoulder.

'How could we utilise them?' said Penny.

'Professor James?' said Ian.

The professor's mind was already grinding away like a ceaseless mill in a fast-flowing river, how could they harness their new discoveries and utilise them to get to Mars?

'Ian is right, the only way is some kind of vehicle and if these plants are as hardy as I think, all we need to do is line the inside with them and we should get oxygen a plenty. The only thing we cannot be certain of is how long they will last for but as they have not shown any sign of decomposition the likelihood is that they shall suffice.

Further to that I am thinking we could create some kind of airtight suit and maybe use a water tank to test them. We could lower someone in and pull them back out, that way if they are air and water tight we know they are strong enough for adventure. Also we could line the helmet with plants and stay underwater in the tank, as soon we prove that we can breathe in them then we should have the capability to walk about on the planet surface.' said Professor James.

'Incredible.' said Penny with her mouth open.

'Inconceivable.' said Professor Giles.

'There is more that I have neglected to tell you regarding the plants.'

Professor James looked at Ian.

'Is there not something else missing from this room. Needed tools or apparatus for the maintenance of any plant?' said Ian waving his hands around the room.

'Water.' Penny exclaimed.

'You mean to tell us that these plants have never been watered?'

'That is correct Giles these plants have never been watered.'

Penny walked over to one of the huge pots and put her hand in the dirt.

'Uncle James come and look.'

Professor James took a handful of soil up with his hand and held it up.

'You are sure that you never watered this soil.'

'Not since putting it in that pot a year ago.'

44

'It is moist and healthy as if it has just been watered. It's almost as if the plants are feeding the soil.'

'This is most interesting think what it could do for agriculture.' said Giles examining the leaves. 'It has veins like a plant from Earth but the fundamentals are different.'

'It does not require oxygen or sunlight. A most perplexing mystery.' said Ian.

'You mean it doesn't need to photosynthesise?' said Giles.

'Appears so.' replied Ian.

'Without the requirement of water this plant could last the duration of our trip with considerable ease.' said Professor James pulling out a pipe and a tobacco pouch.

'It would not surprise me if this plant could outlive us all.' said Ian.

'At the moment it certainly seems plausible.' said Professor James filling his pipe. 'Let us return and have some refreshment upstairs, we have much to discuss.'

They regrouped at the kitchen table with a large pot of tea. They discussed the possibilities and all agreed that in theory it was possible to travel in space. With the properties of the meteorite being able to stand entry into the Earth's atmosphere, the harshness of space and the plant life that seemed to thrive in all conditions, the only thing they would have to worry about is food and water.

'But how long would it take to get us there?' asked Penny putting another sugar in her tea.

'A long time maybe years.' said Professor James.

'Therein lies the primary problem.' said Ian.

'Also the landing maybe tricky. If we just plummet into the ground the crash would probably kill us all even if the craft remained undamaged by the impact.' said Giles.

'And how would we get back?'

'That at least I can answer Penny. If my projections are accurate then the fuel will hardly have been touched by the time we get to Mars. In theory we should be able to launch the same way we did from Earth.'

'Oh yes silly me.'

'You are not silly Penny. Every angle must be covered time and time again.'

'Thank you Uncle James.'

'I have a thought about the landing. Do you all know what a parachute is?' said Professor James.

'By Jove I do, it is a canopy to prevent injury if one jumps from a building or bridge, it was invented by that French chap *Louis-Sébastien Lenormand* if I recall correctly.' said Giles.

'That sounds a pretty pointless invention.'

'I was thinking that Ian.' said Penny.

'It has considerable merit for us, its purpose is to stop things from being damaged when falling from a height, hitherto I would agree that it is hard to think of a use for such a thing but as we shall be falling a great distance, it would solve the problem of impact upon landing.'

'How does it work?' said Ian.

'It is perhaps easier if I draw one. Penny, pass me a pen and paper please?'

'*Leonardo da Vinci* designed one in the late fourteen hundred's if I remember correctly.' said Giles.

'Hold there, Gentleman.' said Ian disappearing into his study and after some loud rummaging returned with a book in his hand. 'Here, I have a scientific copy of *Da Vinci's* works, it should be in there and hopefully in pictorial format.'

Professor James took the beautiful large book that was bound by red leather and gently flicked the pages. 'Success, I found it.' said he turning the book to his interlocutors.

'You are telling me people drop objects using these contraptions?' said Penny.

'They also drop themselves.' said Giles.

'Insanity prevails surely?'

'I am with you on that Penny.' said Ian.

'This picture does it no justice, they are no longer that shape and have greatly improved. There is no reason why we cannot create and test our own.' said Professor James.

'Hurrah, now that's an adventure,' said Giles.

'Quite. Penny, Ian, you still look gravely concerned. The theory holds up.' said Professor James picking up a piece of paper that Penny had put on the table and watching it glide to the floor on currents of air.

'Think about the sail of a ship.' said Giles the wind propels a whole ship forward and at considerable speed. It is the same principle, we use the sail to collect the air and to slow us down as we are falling through it, due to gravity.'

'Now you have explained it like that it makes a lot more sense.' said Penny.

'I agree but we will require some rigorous testing. Remember there will be four of us.' said Ian.

'And that design needs improving I am thinking maybe conical if we are trying to collect air.'

'*Leonardo* not good enough for you Penny?' said Giles.

Professor James and Ian laughed.

'We need to be careful if we are falling at such speed. What is to stop the parachutes from being ripped apart by the force instead of opening and slowing us down.'

'Confound it, how right you are.' said Giles 'In fierce storms we have to take the sails down as they can rip due to the sheer force of the winds.'

'We shall have to engineer thorough testing.' said Ian.

Professor James leant back in his chair and breathed in a large mouthful of tobacco smoke from his glowing pipe.

'Penny can you note down all these points, we need to look at the feasibility, work load and expected schedule required for each component of the mission. To clarify we are all thinking of a craft to carry us that is protected by the meteorite in its entirety and propelled by burning sections of it?'

'Yes, but it will be quite a task to undertake with just the four of us, Professor.' said Giles.

'We are all capable.' said Ian.

'You forget I have helped build boats to sail all the seas of the world, it is surprising the amount of manpower you need just to build a boat, let alone sail one.' said Giles.

'But we are not building a boat.' said Penny.

'No but the same principles apply. We will need to build a capsule big enough for us to essentially live in, not just travel in, we cannot sit in one seat the whole journey as we maybe away for months in space.'

'Are you saying what I think you are saying, Giles?'

'It depends what you think I am saying, Penny?'

'That we need to build a space ship?'

'A space ship? That does not sound right.' said Professor Oakley.

'Yes but she is right we would need to be able to traverse the craft otherwise our joints will cease. This maybe a rather bigger operation than we first envisaged.'

'We cannot build a huge ship without drawing unwanted attention.' said Ian.

'I think we should call in some help, myself and Giles know some trustworthy characters who would oblige, then together we work on building a capsule to get us into the sky and perhaps into space. When we assured the technology works then we can return to Earth and build a ship perhaps get some official outside help if needs be.'

'Shall we need extra hands to build a capsule uncle?'

'Yes Penny, we must construct it out of steel or iron if we are to have any chance.'

'I will draft up some letters tonight. In the meantime let us work on the design. We will need at least six seats and plenty of room to manoeuvre. It would be advisable to have numerous exit points in case of emergency and let us not forget the craft could land any way up.'

'Splendid thinking.' said Ian finishing the last of his beer.

'Are we all agreed that the craft should be conical in shape?'

'Yes Professor, it certainly needs to be aero dynamic.' said Ian.

'Do not forget we need to steer so it may be better to have the backside of it protected. If we can have the airflow run over the back of it and then rudders of some description.'

Professor James took a pencil and started drawing a schematic. They agreed to keep the space to a minimum but enough for them to move about and to be free enough to carry out any repair or tinkering mid-flight. They decided to double line the outside of the ship and put a covering to make a floor, then to use a pulley system of steel strings to steer the rudders, they also designed wings to use as brakes or help steer them but decided that it could be too dangerous as the bracket would be a weakness and could compromise the entire hull.

Penny's chutes it was agreed would come from the back and there would have to be at least four to six, they would only be used in a planet's atmosphere. They also planned to put some more parachutes in reserve, figuring that once they had re-entered and if they were still plummeting too fast, it was possible they could devise a way to throw some more out.

The one thing they had to be certain of was that the entire ship was completely covered in meteorite. They discussed the problem of windows as they would need to see to navigate.

They turned to the inside of the craft and immediately had to rescale as they had forgotten storage. They realised that they already had a hold beneath the floor due to the agreed upon oval design of the ship. The group decided to put hatches along the centre of capsule so they could go into the floor and retrieve whatever they need. This had the tumultuous bonus of them also being able to reach the pulley system in case one of the wires snapped.

It was agreed to put a window in the front so they could all see out but would address the problem of it withstanding the pressure later on. The hours passed, the pencil was sharpened numerous times and Professor James felt his hand cramp.

Finally they had a finished schematic in their hands.

'What shall we call it?' said Giles.

'What do you mean?'

'Every ship has to have a name.'

'Oakley's Rocket?' said Penny.

'Not too sure about that Penny.' replied Professor James.

'The Mad Professor.' said Ian.

VI The Mad Professor

'What a brilliant and apt name, that is the last laugh indeed Ian, well done.' said Professor James.

'Yes, I thought you would chuckle.' replied he.

'Well, I do not think it is a nice name. It's mocking.'

'Indeed it is Penny but not to Ian. The name is ironic for he is anything but as the world shall discover.'

'Well, I still don't like it,' Penny turned and looked at Ian 'but I see that it makes you happy.'

'Yes it does Penny, very happy indeed, so happy that I think it is celebration time, we deserve it and tomorrow we must begin our preparation in earnest.'

'And we must draw up a supply list as soon as possible so we can start to plot the cost and time frames.' said Giles.

The evening passed quickly and they soon found themselves compiling an exhaustive list of required supplies. It was agreed that the two aides they would send for would initially stay in London and source the sheet metal and intricate parts that they could not build themselves. Ian immediately set about building a model of the craft they would make whilst Penny started working on fabrics for the parachute. Once she had finished she was to try some chemistry experiments with the meteorite.

After the model was constructed, they tied chutes to the back of it and dropped it out of an upstairs window taking careful notice of the position it landed in and how much its descent slowed. They all agreed the experiment was hardly fool proof but it allowed them to envisage the dangers that lay ahead and the troubles they may face.

They turned back to the initial building of the ship and pondered what could be done whilst they awaited the arrival of the steel and iron sheets and girders. It was Penny who suggested that they could build the seats, reasoning that they were as important as anything else and would allow them to measure the craft around them.

They built six seats with arm rests and vastly padded backs and bottoms, there were pouches either side for storage and vital supplies such as water, they would also put some plants down there. It was a week later that the first shipment arrived, the place already looked like a factory rather than a home in the week that they had been there, scrap was scattered all over the yard and strange lights emitted from the barn at all hours. Together they worked on creating more of the meteorite meaning they had to keep on purchasing more milk.

Professor James wrote to the University for a grant assuring them that the rewards would be tenfold but by now his reputation was such that he did not even have to ask. Professor James kept receipts meticulously and recorded what they ordered and what they spent.

They were all in the back garden area having a tea break when the horses and carts arrived with the girders and sheets, slowly the frame of the ship came in to view, they tested the size of the seats in the frame and the realisation that this was actually going to happen entered their minds.

As they stood gathered around it the two new trusted assistants showed up.

'Giles, you know Gilbert and Dennis.' said Professor James.

Gilbert looked his pristine self, clean shaven with perfectly parted grey hair and a nice suit whilst Dennis had let his red hair grow out and looked a little dishevelled as was the usual.

'Ha, I was wondering who he sent for, he would not tell me the rascal, I could not have asked for two more splendid fellows.' cried Giles.

'Professor Lincoln it has been a while.' said Dennis leaning forward and shaking Giles' hand.

'Too long young Dennis and how are you these days?'

'I'm fine thank you, learning more and more under Gilbert's tutelage.'

'Nonsense boy you are perfectly capable.' replied he.

'And of course you both know Penny.'

'Yes hallo Penny.' said Gilbert.

'How are you Penny, it has been a few years, you have grown up.'

'So have you Dennis.' replied she brushing her hair behind her ears.

'You have arrived at precisely the right moment gentleman for we have our first sheet ready to go on the frame.'

'Professor Oakley it is a pleasure to make your acquaintance,'

'We have met before Doctor Gilbert but it was a long time ago and please call me Ian.'

'Forgive me for I do not recall Ian. This is Dennis a very promising student.'

'A pleasure.' said he offering his hand. 'Forgive me for being so forward, if you are not too tired from your journey, I have the first sheet ready to go on the frame.'

'Nonsense, we are not tired, of course we shall assist.' ejaculated Dennis.

'Yes let's and then you can fill us in on all that has occurred, your letter was cryptic, you confided that we were to work on some kind of craft and the curiosity has plagued me every night since I received your letter.'

'Apologies it was too sacred to write albeit there would scarcely be a resident on this entire island that would believe it.'

'Believe what?' cried Dennis.

'That we are going to Mars.' replied Ian.

The two newcomers did not laugh but stood with mouths agape.

'After we have fitted the new sheets there is something I have to show you. I have an exciting development in my experimentations.'

'What is that my dear Penny?'

'Oh you just wait until you see uncle.'

'Well let us see to this first,' said Giles.

The guests dropped their cases where they were and as they entered the barn were immediately taken back by the sight of the craft. They stood there stumped and as the green glow filled their eyes Professor James wondered whether they might have come over catatonic. It was Penny who snapped them out of it demanding that they had plenty of time to take it all in but her discovery at that moment was of the greatest importance.

She led them to her workbench that she had fashioned for herself alongside Ian's.

'What is it Penny?' asked Dennis.

'Well I think I may have solved the problem of having windows.'

'The windows?' asked Gilbert.

'Must we do this now. Our poor guests have no information as of yet.'

'I cannot wait uncle, this is so exciting, you shall see.'

'We are a quick study Professor James.'

'I know that Gilbert but still.'

'Nonsense.' replied he.

'Very well then.' said he.

'In order to traverse space we need windows in the craft for viewing purposes. I was doubtful that normal glass would hold up so I set about creating a double thick pane of glass when a thought occurred to me, is it possible to create something out of the meteorite itself? It is transparent and we can use milk to manipulate it so why not break it down to a molecular level? I decided to heat it with some milk and then cool it back down in its combined state but rather than leave it as lump, I smeared it into a small smooth pane.

'Very good Penny what did you discover?' said Professor James.

'I realised it was clear enough to see through but if my theory was correct it should have retained some key properties. Who would like to be my guest?' said she holding up a lump hammer.

'I will.' said Gilbert walking forward.

'You see that plate of green glass there, I want you to smash it with this hammer, as hard as you can?'

'As hard as I can. Are you sure?'

'Absolutely, when it shatters into smithereens do not worry yourself as it is part of the experiment.' replied Penny.

The Doctor brought the lump hammer down as hard as he could with a mighty swing but the hammer just bounced off it.

'Splendid. Look not even a scratch on it. We have our window.'

'Incredible.' said Ian walking forward and picking up the glass to examine it. 'This is amazing; not even a scratch.'

'I call it Penny Glass.'

'I assure you it will cost more than a Penny.' said Giles.

'Penny, please make us a window screen, you have the required measurements.'

'Yes uncle I am on it.'

'To be certain, triple the thickness off the glass. The thicker the better as long as we retain the visual element of it.'

'Good idea Professor.'

'Yes, clever thinking.' said Dennis.

'We have no way to test the impact of space itself so caution would be prudent.'

'Indeed.' added Giles.

'Now come we must fit this sheet of metal.' cried Ian.

They hammered, clanged and thudded for the next hour until eventually the first sheet of metal was warped and melded into shape. They took their guests into the house and divulged everything they knew hitherto, watching their mouths drop wider with each passing sentence.

As the weeks passed, all the panels got applied and they installed the back end and then finally the rudders. Penny finished the chutes, they tucked them all up and attached special wires to deploy them from inside the cabin. They installed the floor and the chairs and were finally climbing in and out of the capsule. All they had to do was install Penny's windscreen and cover the whole craft with meteorite. They decided on a plate to cover the windshield in case it weakened over time, the ship would have a sliding shield covered in meteorite that they could bring down.

The next thing they had to design was the suit, it was almost overlooked and for the test flight they wondered whether they needed them. It was unanimously decided that it was a fool hardy risk not to wear them so they constructed a huge vat, 9 ft tall, 6ft wide and filled it with water. They used the strongest material they could find and then Professor James had the idea of applying a very thin coat of the milk and meteor mixture. The plan worked and they discovered that the material was extremely tough and fire proof.

The construction of the helmet was the most difficult thing but again with their new wonder potion they worked to create it. They lined the entire helmet with the extra-terrestrial plant leaves and worked to create a water tight suit. It was Dennis who was the first to test it in the tank and he nearly drowned, they hauled him out by the ropes that was attached to him, he was spitting up water and choking. The failure was the suit not the plants. They dried the suit out and tried again but the initial experiment was not a waste of time as they realised that all the suits would have to be individually tested to avoid anyone being accidentally killed.

They knew this was just an initial test flight but Professor James insisted that they acted as if it was the departure for Mars 'our lives may depend on it' he said many times.

Professor James was almost giddy with excitement at their forthcoming adventure yet he did not reveal it in anyway. He knew the scientific discoveries that lay ahead were vast and the possibilities somehow managed to eclipse the discoveries they had made so far.

The second tank test was successful and after being lifted out, Dennis went down into the tank again and agreed to yank the rope to signal that he was ok. Once he landed at the bottom, he would yank the rope once when he wanted to return to the surface of his own choice but if he yanked the rope twice then this was an indication that he was in trouble.

After an hour had passed they began to worry and yanked the rope, they got a yank back. On the wooden platform that surrounded the tank Ian and Professor James asked Penny to fetch them some playing cards, they sat chatting away playing *gin* wondering if Dennis was ever going to yank the cord, finally after nearly three hours they felt a sharp yank and began to haul him up.

When they interviewed Dennis, it turned out that he had managed to fall asleep despite the plant's stimulating properties, they laughed and congratulated him then one by one they all went down into the tank with their suits on. Professor James insisted upon this to get some preparation of being in an alien environment where your life depended on the suit. He made a mental note that the suits could possibly be used for deep sea exploration.

Eventually all the suits were tested and ready. Professor James stood there with Professors Oakley, Gilbert and Lincoln along with Penny and Dennis and smiled. He announced that they were ready for trial flight but must pack as if they were off on the main voyage. This was the only way to conduct a proper test.

They discussed and argued the merits of all of them going aboard should not at least two of them stay behind to carry on the cause in case of failure. It was then argued that perhaps only one of them should go, that way they would lose only one team member and the rest could try again.

As a group they were all of stout scientific ignorance when it came to adventures of science so it was agreed that they would either all perish or all triumph together. The list of supplies had already been made and they already had a majority of them in storage, they used all non-perishables as they would need their food to keep and stuck mainly to canned goods. They packed the entire hull, one side was beer, as it was safer to drink than water, the other side was food and extra tools, ropes and wires.

It was Giles who raised the question of protection and advised that they have an armoury. Professor James agreed and required six spare guns, swords and daggers to be stored in separate places in case of discovery by a trespasser.

They stood back and inspected the Mad Professor, it shone a beautiful emerald green, pleased with what they had created they embraced each other and shook one another's hand. They discussed when they would launch and agreed that they did not want it to be seen but it should be in daylight so they could see the Earth and in case of an emergency landing they could try and plot a course. Giles warned that by use of parachute there would be little chance of being able to control their descent. Dawn the day after the morrow was what they agreed on. For now they would celebrate by going in to town to drink and eat as much as money could buy.

They spent the next day in preparation and most of the afternoon putting on their suits and practicing getting in and out of the Mad Professor. They practiced opening every hatch including the emergency ones. Professor James even had them do it blind folded warning they should all be able to move about the ship quickly and without hinderance if they are to survive. His statement added some gravitas to the proceedings and each individual sought their own solace to reflect on the fact that they might not be breathing on the morrow if this test run failed.

As evening approached they inspected each other over the dining room table and tried to read each other's fears. The excitement mixed with peril created an exciting, addictive yet dangerous cocktail. Now that it was upon them so they feared for their life all the more, would they explode instantaneously and become another crater in the field with nothing to explain or acknowledge their great feats? Oh what calamity it is to explore the unknown; to be on the forefront of science.

VII Test Run

In the early hours they assembled in the kitchen and after breakfast the party began their final preparations for a trip into space. Professor James made everyone put some essentials into their uniforms, they each had a large leaf of the meteor plant that will hopefully give them enough emergency oxygen should it be required. They also put a knife in a sheath that had been specially created by Professor James as they may need to cut themselves free or the can openers maybe lost. He also made them pack some rations into their pockets, in all probability it was either death or success but he was determined to cover every eventuality especially as his niece's life was at stake. If the capsule crashed back to Earth they might become marooned but whatever happened they would be prepared.

Once they were sure they had everything they went into the stables, stirred the horses and then using eight of them dragged the ship out of its hiding place to the scaffold they had built.

They heaved and pushed in the morning darkness to the scaffold they had prepared deep into the meadow. It was too much of a risk to locate it near the house that contained all their precious research. After ninety minutes of solid graft they were in position. Professor James opened the door of the capsule.

'I believe this honour is yours, Ian.'

'Thank you old friend but I require another promise from you all?'

'What is that?' asked Giles mopping his brow with an old torn handkerchief.

'I want you to promise me that if we ever get to Mars, whether it be the next time we go or on our tenth mission, you will allow me to be the first person to set foot on the red planet.'

'Not one of us would think any different.' cried Gilbert.

'Come, let us get inside we are already late the sun is up and it will not be long before people are walking their dogs and such.'

'Yes, you are right Professor James let us get in.'

They climbed aboard, it was difficult to get into the seat at the perpendicular angle at which they found themselves, but eventually everyone was in. Professors James and Oakley were in the front whilst Giles and Dennis were on the back row leaving Gilbert and Penny in the middle.

'Ok, everybody check, you should have water and spare plants in the right hand side of your chairs, in the left hand side should be a supply of weapons and first aid along with notebooks and pencils. The hatch is secured, we do not know what will happen so if you want to step out, now is the time, remember we could just explode here and now.'

There was a still silence.

'What about you Penny? We could do with an observer on the ground.'

'No chance at all I am a scientist on this trip not your niece remember.'

'Worth a try, if we survive this I rather expect your father is going to have words with me.'

There was a small chuckle from the others.

Professor James closed his eyes and said a small prayer, then he let his thoughts go free and put any fears to the back of his mind, he was a scientist this was his duty, he opened his eyes and felt calm. He looked up at the green screen and the sky so beautiful through the green hue. 'You have to leave now.' his instinct screamed at him out of nowhere.

'Gentleman we are out of time, this is it, on my mark we ignite, strap yourself in and hold on.'

'What if we need the toilet?' asked Penny.

'Confound it child, you had to think of something, didn't you?' said Professor James.

They all looked at each other but Professor James was really annoyed that they had overlooked something so big, he spun the dynamo handle as hard as he could to charge up enough electricity to ignite the booster chunks of meteorite.

'We shall not be long in any case.' said he hitting the ignition button.

The question of them exploding into a million pieces was soon answered as they were pinned back to their chairs with such immense force that they thought their skulls would implode and splinter the backs of their chairs with bone shrapnel.

Professor James could not believe the force with which his face was being pushed back, he was glad that they had insisted on reinforcing the chairs but even so he was certain they were all about to be smashed through the back of the vehicle. He struggled to turn his neck and saw his old friend Ian with his skin pulled back so tight against his skull that Professor James could see a bizarre caricature of his friend as a youngster and the glee in his eyes was undeniable.

Professor James looked out of the window and saw the clouds quickly giving way and the sky turning ever darker shades of green. There was an immense rumble as the ship powered its way through the Earth's atmosphere, they saw space, stars and the moon but all were green due to their protectant glass. The screen turned transparent like glass as if it had been reading their thoughts.

'It must have been the Earth's atmosphere that turned it green.' said Ian through gritted teeth.

Professor James did not answer as he was trying to reach the lever in front of him to slow the craft, it was hard to move his arms and he realised that only someone strong could pilot it. He felt the pull easing off now they were in space and wondered why as the propulsion should be the same given that they had not turned any of the thrusters off. He managed to grab the lever and the craft slowed considerably.

'Look its space!' cried Penny.

'Hurrah.' shouted Giles.

'Hurrah indeed.' added Ian wiping his eye.

'What a fine day this is for science and for mankind, we will party tonight like man never has before and then we shall set about taking our trip to Mars.'

'So everything is acceptable then?'

'We are alive aren't we Giles?'

'Do not be insolent Penny.' said Professor James.

'Do the brakes actually work? We are still travelling exceptionally fast from what I can see.' said Dennis.

Professor James unclipped his belt and walked over to the screen.

'We are aren't we.' said he.

'What is wrong?'

'I am not sure Ian, something does not feel right, we have not slowed down enough to drop the gravitational force as much as this, unless it is simply the fact that we are in outer space.'

'It must be old man, waters feel different in the same ship, a tropical ocean sails vastly different to a cold one.' said Giles.

'Could be.' replied Professor James.

'Look at the plants.' yelled Penny.

Professor James looked up at the plants that lined the ship and saw it was as if they were holding hands, the leaves had stretched themselves out to create one protective inner layer.

Giles got up and walked to the front and looked out of the window, Professor James moved to the back of the ship to allow them room and motioned to Penny and the others to have their turn, they took a minute or two each, looking out into the starry scape of the unknown and mysterious. They knew the significance of the occasion.

'Come everybody let us return to our seat there is something I want to show you.' said Professor James grabbing the steering controls.

He was relieved when the craft responded as it should and began turning. As the capsule turned a huge bright blue sphere came into view, it had a large sprawling of green upon it with white on the top and bottom respectively. One by one they realised that they were looking at their home.

'If I dropped dead now I would be grateful that I was allowed to see that.' said Giles.

'Myself as well.' said Gilbert.

'We should charge people for trips; we would make an absolute fortune.' said Dennis.

'Yes, I suspect we would.' laughed Ian.

Once again they took it in turns having their view.

'We have seen enough and I am not keen for us to over extend our confidence. Let us return after this and prepare for our main mission.'

'We have only just arrived James I shall not hear of it.' said Ian.

'I am in agreement.' said Gilbert.

Giles shook his head while Penny put her hand on her hips like she always did when she got upset.

'Ok let us cruise around the Earth for a little longer but you wanted me to lead the team so I am going to lead it. I will be turning back for home soon.'

'We are still moving way too fast Professor James, look how far away we are past Earth already, we need to be careful it's getting smaller.' said Dennis.

'Ok.' said Professor James returning to his seat and grabbing the controls.

Penny yawned and stretched her arms. Her eyes opened wide with terror.

'Why am I tired? The plants should be giving us amplified oxygen.'

'The plants. They're changing colour.' cried Gilbert.

Professor James looked up and saw that the plants were slowly changing orange.

'They must be dying.' said Ian.

'But we need them to breathe!' cried Dennis.

'Professor James Bedford we need to get out of trouble.' said Giles.

'I know. Hang on.' he replied grabbing the controls and swinging them back towards Earth. 'Gilbert can you work out how much time we have from the second that the plants stop giving out oxygen.'

'On it, where are the schematics of the craft?'

'I have them.' said Giles.

Giles and Dennis held out the large piece of paper in front of Gilbert so he could scrawl the measurements on his notepad and begin to calculate.

'I will need time but at a quick guess Professor three days maybe four.'

'Blast us back to Earth.' cried Dennis.

'Steady on.' said Ian.

'Uncle James I feel really tired.'

'Hang on.' said Professor James. As he grappled with the thrusters he saw Penny slump in her chair. '*Penny, my God, my sweet Penny hang on.*'

'Professor James it is no good we are runni ...' Giles slumped forward as well.

'Look.' cried Dennis, 'the plants are exuding some kind of miasma.'

'Confound it, I feel tired as well, must stay awake.'

'Professor James are we dying?'

'I pray not Gilbert but it would seem the oxygen is evaporating as the plants decay.'

'It makes no sense my calculations show that we should have at least another two days at the bare minimum.'

'We obviously don't.' said Dennis falling into unconsciousness.

Gilbert and Professor James looked at each other with a solemn gaze.

'It has been an honour.' said Gilbert succumbing to the darkness.

Professor James slapped himself around the face, he looked up at his darling niece slumped on her seat and felt tears forming in his eyes. I have murdered my kin, you bloody fool, why can you not just stay at home. Professor James noticed the craft was turning away from Earth, he had not yet hit the accelerator yet the thrusters suddenly ignited and he saw they were now hurtling through space. He tried in vain to grab the controls but he couldn't, he had no strength left and his head was lolling from the lack of oxygen. Professor James made one last effort to grab the control stick like an opium addict grasping for one last hit on the pipe. It was of no use and the cold black existence of a death in space grabbed him from his chair and took him into oblivion.

Death, was always the one adventure that a scientist was ultimately curious about, one that he always dreamed of coming back from and Professor James was no exception. It was the sensation of being aware of the darkness, of the nothingness, trapped inside your own eternal space. The universe was supposed to be outside of you but perhaps all along it had been within the whole time. Professor James felt like he was an explorer in a space suit drifting through the realms of emptiness, the darkness grew bright and all he could see was orange. Slowly as he fumbled around in his soul his senses began to detect something, he could feel the top of his thighs and buttocks, they were touching a comfy surface, he was in a chair, the orange light came rushing towards him and he opened his eyes.

'We're alive, confound it, we're all alive.' cried he jumping out of his chair and racing to Penny, he gently shook her, she stirred and looked up.

'Oh Uncle James I thought we perished.'

'So did I my sweet child.' replied he placing his hand on her soft warm cheek.

The others also started stirring.

'We're alive Hurrah!' cried Giles.

'Hurrah!' echoed Dennis.

'Hurrah!' they all cried in unison.

'This is most extraordinary.' said Gilbert putting on his glasses.

'That plant when it turned orange was exuding some kind of chemical gas, I swear it.' said Dennis.

'You think we were knocked unconscious?' said Giles.

'It gets weirder than that I am afraid. Just before I went under the ship turned itself away from Earth and the boosters kicked in despite me not having pressed the button. And given it is a pulley system it seems unlikely that a delayed reaction could have been created, it will either work or it won't.'

'You are correct Professor James. I built the thing myself.' replied Giles uncorking a beer and having a sip.

'The question I would like to know is how long have we been out for and further more how far have we travelled? I feel most peculiar as if I have slept for a very long time.' said Penny.

'Yes, I feel like I have certainly had some good rest.' said Professor James.

'Well that is easy.' said Gilbert pulling out his stopwatch 'We left about five thirty am and it's now eight-thirty.'

'Am or pm?' asked Dennis.

'What day?' asked Ian.

'Confound it. We do not know do we?' cried Gilbert.

'And we cannot tell by the outside either.' said Professor Oakley.

Professor James stood up and walked to the window.

'I fear that we are lost deep in space.'

Giles walked to the front and stood by him. 'Confound it, there must be a way we can see where we are, if we can navigate our way across the oceans, we can do the same with the sky, surely?'

'We need a team of erudite scientists and that is just what we are.' said Professor James with a shallow grin.

'Splendid.' cried Gilbert slapping his thigh. 'This really is turning out to be quite the adventure.

'The north star.' said Penny. 'let us see if we can find the north star then we shall have some bearing.

'Excellent idea Penny.' said James. 'Who is the best in astrology here?'

'That would be my field.' said Ian.

'Then come up and see if you can see the North star or a constellation that looks familiar.' said Giles.

'Before you do I have an idea. Giles when I slow us right down please turn us on our axis three hundred and sixty degrees.'

'Why?' asked Dennis.

'Because we maybe right above Earth just looking out of the wrong window.' answered Giles.

'Ha indeed.' said Professor James 'That is why you are the explorer, simple logic, there is nothing to say that we have not been flying in circles although I would be surprised.'

'So would I but we still need to rule it out.' said Giles.

'Quite.' replied Professor James.

Professor James grabbed the controls and applied the brakes, this time the craft did exactly as it was instructed and slowed. The ship began to turn and all they saw were stars until a huge red planet filled their periphery.

'Good God that is not Earth.' cried Dennis.

'Unless we have travelled through time.' ventured Giles.

'Highly unlikely.' said Penny.

'I recognise the huge volcano on its face. That is Olympus Mons.' said Ian.

'And Olympus Mons is on Mars.' said Gilbert.

'Quite.' replied Professor James.

'By Jove I do not believe it.' said Ian.

'By Mars actually.' said Giles with a wry smile.

'But how?' cried Dennis.

'That I do not know, it seems to be most odd and I am not a believer in coincidence.' replied Professor James.

'You mean we were brought here?'

'Correct Penny. Scientific certainty predicts that there is no conceivable possibility that we set off for a short trip in space, fall asleep and then wake up parked right outside Mars which is where we dreamed of going.'

'I agree it all seems spurious.' said Gilbert.

'Why did you pick Mars Ian?' said Dennis.

'Because as far as I could tell by the trajectory that is where the meteor came from.'

'Bloody hell Ian and you wait until now to tell us that?'

'Didn't think to Professor.' said Ian reaching for a hip flask and getting out of his seat.

'These plants have some hidden soporific quality to them.' said Professor James.

'And they have returned to normal.' said Dennis pushing his red hair aside to see clearly.

'Capable of everything we need, sleep and energy, I am feeling really energised and it is their oxygen I have no doubt.' said Ian.

'I am of a lively disposition as well.' said Gilbert scrawling in his notebook.

'How long do you think we were unconscious for?' asked Dennis.

'There is no way of telling whether it is night or day but it is half past the hour of five at the moment?' said Penny.

'And what day is it?'

'You mean we could have been asleep for days?' said Dennis.

'Gilbert has a point. We do not know what day it is. This plant has many qualities unknown to us and as it is extra-terrestrial we cannot apply the limitation of Earth based plants upon it. What if this plant is so powerful that it can sustain life. Perhaps the properties that it exudes are enough to feed us. We could have been asleep for weeks.'

'Or perhaps just hours?' said Professor Oakley.

'That is plausible yet there is one factor that lends itself to my former proposal.'

'What is that uncle?'

'How long does it take to get to Mars?'

There was silence in the room as they all looked out at the Red planet.

'Months.' said Giles.

'More like years.' replied Gilbert. 'I really did not think we would get very far, my expectation was to get near space and then figured that we would have to descend. The theory held which is why I gave it my all but rarely does science work in practice without decades of good luck.'

'This craft is the fastest thing we have known and much faster than any device previously designed by man but can it really be that fast to get us to Mars in a couple of hours?' said Giles.

'I wonder how long we have been gone?' said Penny.

'There is some evidence that dictates that we could not have been asleep for months or years.'

'What is that?' asked Gilbert.

'Our fingernails and facial hair.'

'How clever you are Professor James.' cried Ian. 'Our fingernails would have grown and we would all have beards.'

Penny gave a shallow cough.

'With the exception of Penny of course.' said Ian.

This made Giles guffaw.

'I am glad you are so thorough Professor.'

'Why is that Dennis?'

'Because you made us pack as if we really were going meaning that we have all our food and supplies with us.'

'Yes we do. We have a multitude of questions that we cannot answer at this moment so perhaps rather than perplexing ourselves with how we came to be here and the complex intricacies of our journey, we should just look at what is right in front of us. Do any of you fancy accompanying myself and Ian to Mars?'

'Hurrah.' shouted Penny.

'No, it is like this Penny, *Hurrah!*' cried Giles in a deep booming voice.

'*Hurrah!*' they all shouted in unison.

'I am to be the first off.' said Ian.

'Let us all get our helmets on just in case something happens upon landing.'

'We are so fortunate to not require them within the craft, do you not think?' said Penny.

'Yes, the science in those plants is staggering to mankind I suspect.' said Dennis closely inspecting the leaves within his helmet.

'Where should we try and land?'

Giles got up and walked to the front. 'I am not sure let me have a look.'

As much as you might know the night sky Giles; perhaps this should be my area.

'Avoid the volcano at all costs there are a lot of storms about it.' said Gilbert.

Ian looked back at Gilbert and shook his head.

'Be my guest.' said Giles.

'There can be storms about Olympus Mons but fear not for that is not where we are going. Professor James follow me.' said Ian wiping his hand and pointing to the screen. 'Come southeast, I worked it out to be about seven hundred and fifty miles, you see the three dots in a symmetrical line? That is Tharsis Montes and the middle one is Parvonis Mons.'

'Peacock Mountain.'

'Well done professor, I see you can remember your Latin, those three mountains are way bigger than anything on Earth, the other two are called Arsia and Ascraeus Mons.'

'Arsia, what is that in Latin?' said Gilbert.

'I am thinking it could be a reference to the mighty forest that used to stand outside Rome, Arsia Silva.' said Dennis.

'Silva is Latin for wood so your theory is probably accurate.' said Ian.

'Someone has a taste for the theatrical; don't they Penny?'

'What do you mean Professor James?'

'I mean what is the reference in the word Ascraeus?'

'Confound it, I know, I am sure of it.'

'Penny you better have been doing your studies. You will not be coming along if you cannot learn your studies.'

'Uncle James you are embarrassing me.' said Penny pinching her eyes. 'It is not a word, it is a name and I am pretty sure it is a place not a person.'

'Brilliant Penny, I will give you a small aid, the name is a metonym.'

'Ascraeus … Ascraeus … Rural … Asc … it's Ascra on Mount Helios the birth place of Hesiod the ancient Greek poet.'

'Bravo.' said Giles applauding.

'Nonsense, stop it, you will make me blush, you know I hate it when I blush.'

'Pay attention to Parvonis Mons and come down again on a straight line and at the same angle you did from Olympus to Parvonis.' said Ian.

'Understood.' replied Professor James.

'Now do you see the planet surface is cracked and full of fissures next to the end of that giant scar?'

'Yes, I can see it clearly.'

'Good, that is where we are going to land right at the end of the scar where the fissures begin.'

'What is that scar?'

'That Dennis is Valles Marineris. A canyon so vast it would stretch from one side of America to the other. Professor James, look at the other end of the canyon, we could fly in through Coprates Chasma and fly straight through the wide section known as Melas Chasma and through to the landing site just above the huge meteor crater discovered by *Jean Oudemans*.'

'How deep is the chasm?' said Giles.

'That is what we do not know I suspect Coprates and Melas to be very deep indeed maybe even incomprehensibly so.'

'Be more specific Ian.' said Professor James.

'Five miles maybe.'

'*Five miles deep*. We need to be careful we do not get lost down it.' said Gilbert.

'He is correct Professor James, we cannot come in too low, we have no idea how deep it is versus how shallow at our proposed landing site.' said Giles.

'Why there though Ian?' said Gilbert.

'It is the best guess I could make. Following the assumption that it had come from Mars this is where it would have likely come from. When I looked at it on the map it seemed a likely place if there was anything on Mars. In between a giant mountain, a huge plain, a gargantuan chasm and an enormous crater you have all the options the planet has to offer.'

'Thinking about it that is where I would settle.' said Dennis.

'I agree.' said Giles.

'Quite.' said Professor James.

'What about hurricanes Ian?' cried Penny.

'You are thinking of Jupiter.' said Professor James.

'I believe she is, there are vortices on Mars as well albeit they are way to the north and dissipate quickly.'

'Is there anything else we need to know Ian.' said Giles eating some bread and brushing the crumbs off his jacket.

Ian tapped his finger on his chin. 'Yes there is. Dust storms. A dust storm on Mars can cover the whole planet and it would be suicide to attempt to enter or to leave during one.

'Let us put the plan into action then before a reason comes along to hinder our progress.'

Professor James felt a twinge of anxiety in his stomach and tried to ignore it. He could not afford to be anxious about their descent as it would detract from his concentration. Yet he could not escape the question that was gnawing away at him like a maggot on a corpse; would they survive the crash?

VIII The First Man to Mars

They resumed their seats and Professor James ignited the ship, they travelled at a slower pace and sat in silence, each one of them taking in all they could. Mars despite being large in their periphery was still a way off and it took several hours to get to the atmosphere. During that time they passed around sandwiches, cake and beer. There was excited chatter as the party neared their destination.

Professor James gave the order for everyone to brace themselves, the craft rocked violently, they had removed the helmets to eat but now cautiously put them back on. They felt themselves buffeted with ever more violence and they kept praying that the hull would keep its integrity. Through the screen, the shape of Mars warped and changed, the ice caps disappeared and flames of various colours engulfed their capsule as they raced through the atmosphere. They speculated at the possibility of life down there and grew ever more excited about what they were going to find.

Ian explained about the canals that had been spotted by astronomers suggesting there was indeed an alien race living there; presumably farmers of some description that have created irrigation ditches for their crops.

Professor James was focused on the controls throughout. Eventually the craft punched through a pink layer and out into a bright butterscotch coloured sky. They flew down the mighty Coprates and Melas Chasma's. Professor James was finally starting to master the controls and skillfully flew along the nearside canyon edge. He wondered whether his new found skills were a coincidence he could not help but feel that they were being led there.

'Look at all the rocks. It is like a desert.' cried Penny.

'This is the whole planet with the exception of the polar caps.' said Gilbert.

'Giles get ready. I am going to stop the craft. We need to deploy the chutes.'

'Righto.' replied he.

'On my mark three … two … one … now.'

Professor James slammed on the brake and Giles yanked the handle that simultaneously deployed all the chutes. The craft swung, decelerated and as they had forgotten to strap themselves back in, they all fell out of their chairs, the capsule swung violently throwing them around like stones in a rolling barrel. The craft was righted and they began descending to the surface.

'Is everyone ok?' asked Ian.

'I think so.' said Penny.

'My arms are a little bruised but I'll live.' replied Dennis.

'That was quite a tumble that you took there.' said Gilbert.

'I did not fare much better.' said Professor James rubbing his arms and looking out the window. 'We have no way to steer the ship; we are at the mercy of the chutes now.'

'That could be a problem when we return to Earth.' said Giles.

'Yes but at least on Earth if it is too bad we can head for water.' added Dennis.

'I am not sure we would have time to escape if she sunk too quick mind.' said Giles.

'What is that over there?' cried Ian.

'What?' said Gilbert.

'Professor James look, does that look like an entrance to a cave to you?'

'It could be a shadow.'

Ian grabbed his telescope. 'That is no shadow.'

'It looks like we have found somewhere to explore already – Hurrah!' said Giles.

'We are still coming in too fast. Everybody brace yourselves.' said Professor James.

'We are going straight into those rocks. What if the ship does not hold?' cried Penny.

'It is has been sturdy enough so far.' said Ian.

'Yes but we are on Mars so it is not the time to find out.' replied Dennis.

'I agree it is best that we do not tempt fate. I am going to start the boosters at the last minute, we must hope they respond correctly because if one of the boosters fires us straight into the rock then in all likelihood we will be smashed to smithereens.'

Professor James was silent as the craft was plummeting to the rocks below and he had to guess when he should ignite the booster as there was a large patch of sand just past the rocks. The problem was that beyond the sand was another collection of rocks so he had to judge it just right. For the first time he felt perspiration on his forehead.

Hitherto the temperature had been absolutely perfect and the thought nagged him again that this trip had gone just a little too well, even sailing to India was not as problem free as this.

'Now.' he shouted to himself and hit the booster full on, almost immediately he slammed the brake on, they had gained forward momentum and were starting to tilt down again, the surface was getting ever closer and they held their breaths as they saw the Martian surface coming to meet them. They missed the first set of rocks.

'Confound it this going to be close.' said Professor James.

As strong as the armour was he was convinced it could not stand smashing through rock at many hundreds of miles an hour.

The ground was getting ever closer and they were all now buckled into the seats as hard as possible, they gripped tight. The capsule came crashing down and they held on as they felt the home-made safety belts tearing into them. The capsule had hit the soft sand and was gliding straight to the rocks but the momentum was slowing all the time as the jagged meteorite chunks raked through the sand and stopped the Mad Professor just as the rocks approached.

'Are we all ok?' asked Professor James.

'I feel like I have been ripped in half.' said Giles.

'I think that's what we all feel like.' said Ian. 'I cannot believe that we have made it to Mars. We really have done it.'

'Yes we have my old friend and when we leave this craft the honour is all yours.'

'Thank you Jim, you were always a grand friend and it is one of life pleasures that I made your acquaintance.'

'I echo your sentiment, now stop embarrassing us and get your things together, there is much exploring to be had.'

The capsule came to rest at a slanted angle, they all got out of their seats and checked their supplies. Giles suggested that they pack their weapons just in case. They all took some extra leaves and stuffed them in their pockets, then they all collected their marked bag which contained all manner of supplies including food and drink, the idea being that they all wore a survival kit at all times. They did not intend to spend days out at a time but wanted to ensure they could last the duration if it was required.

Professor James looked at his niece and thought how strange it was that he could remember sitting her on his lap when she was little girl and regaling her with stories of adventure and science, how proud he felt when her father brought her around when she was eight and she proudly announced that she was going to be the best female scientist that ever lived. She had certainly shown immense promise since then and Professor James wondered whether she might not live to fulfil her own prophecy. A loud bang as Giles dropped a box brought Professor James back from his pensive stupor.

'Do not forget your helmets they must be air tight or you will die as soon as you step foot outside of the capsule. They checked themselves thoroughly and inspected one another's suits. They checked their revolvers, knives and rations.

'Ian will you kindly open the door and step on to the Martian landscape.' said Professor James.

'Nothing could make me happier.' replied he marching to the door and unscrewing the latch.

He pushed on the door. 'You sealed this well didn't you Giles.'

'We tested it. The door should open without hinderance.'

'Yes it should. I tried the bloody thing twice myself.' said Giles.

'Push harder.' said Dennis.

'And make sure you fully unscrewed it.' added Gilbert.

They saw Ian yank the wheel around as hard he could indicating that it was fully unscrewed. He pushed but it did not move, then he kicked the door and it would not budge so he shoulder barged it and still it held fast.

'It is no use it is stuck.' said Ian kicking the bottom of the door out of frustration.

'Come hither man I will attend to it.' said Professor James.

Ian moved out of the way and Professor James without losing momentum from his walk over to it crashed into the door with his shoulder, there was an almighty crack, the door flew open and Professor James went flying out the door and onto the Martian soil.'

'Sorry Ian do not know my own strength sometimes.' said he returning to his feet. 'I did not meant to steal a glorious moment from you.'

'On the contrary Professor James, you actually gave us all a glorious moment.' replied he laughing heartily.

Professor James looked up and saw they had all gathered around the doorway laughing and sniggering like a bunch of school children. Professor James picked up a handful of sand and let it run through his fingers, it was a strange texture and even the way it fell through his gloved fingers seemed different from Earth.

'The atmosphere must be a lot thinner here for when I fell I hardly felt it.' said Professor James.

'Is that so?' replied Dennis running and jumping from the capsule as hard and high as he could.

Professor James found himself contort with laughter at the look of surprise on Dennis' face as he sailed through the air as if he could fly.

'Incredible, look how far he jumped.' remarked Penny.

'I am next thank you.' said Ian running and jumping out onto the soil.

He struck a pose like someone in a ballet and had them all laughing once more. Once they were all on Martian soil, they were left with the conundrum of how to shut the door of the capsule, that was now left swung open. With great difficulty they managed to help Dennis climb back up, he closed it and secured it with rope to protect it from any sand storms.

They took in their surroundings including the strange moon above them. It appeared so strange to be looking at a moon that was not their own yet Professor James could not help but feel some reassurance that at least they were in their own solar system.

'Come we must start exploring, it looks perfectly safe to walk from the vehicle and these plants are working really well, I am wide awake and full of energy.' said Giles.

'We had noticed.' said Gilbert.

'It is just over yonder. I made a mental note.' said Penny.

'Yes, I saw too, we can walk up that ridge and into the rocks up there.' said Giles.

'Splendid, let us march forth.' said Gilbert.

'Ian you can lead the way.' said Professor James.

The party walked in single file and were for the most part silent as each one contemplated the barren and alien world. They found themselves bounding in large footsteps even uphill. Their energy levels were truly impressive and even after fifteen minutes of marching through oxidised dust and sand they still felt like they had just jumped out of bed after twelve hours of uninterrupted sleep.

'Look there it is.' exclaimed Penny.

'You know it is strange but this ridge now seems rather convenient don't you think?' said Gilbert.

'How do you mean old fellow?' replied Ian.

'I mean that if I didn't know better I would have said it was a path.'

'That is true but there aren't any footprints.' added Dennis.

'No there is not, but there are a lot of sand storms on Mars and that could account for it.' replied Penny.

'Think of the fields back home how many mud tracks there are. You do not see footprints on them.'

'Excellent point Giles.' said Professor James bending over and inspecting the ground. 'Under the loose dust it is feasible that this is a well-worn path but unfortunately could also just be erosion.'

'We are not going home until we find out.' said Ian taking the lead.

As they trudged up the ridge to the entrance of the cave they constantly scanned for signs of life but there was none, not a bird or a bat in the sky, a fox or a rat in the sand and not even an ant or a worm in the soil. There was an eerie silence that made it all the more unsettling as if Mars had been deserted for some ungodly reason. Professor James thought of it as a Ghost planet.

'Perhaps we are just making wishful conjectures and there is no such life.' said Dennis.

'We will find out.' said Giles lifting his eyes in his faceplate to scan the horizon once again.

'If there is life it will not be on the surface as we would have seen movement from space, we covered swathes of the planet in our descent and would have seen any herds of grazing beasts or moving populations.' said Gilbert.

As the expeditioners approached the cave entrance they realised that what seemed to be a small cave was more akin to a large cavern. They stood beneath it looking into the dark abyss.

'Are you sure this is wise?'

'Fear not Penny, we are explorers, fear is our territory, for all things that are unknown to man is what people fear.' said Giles.

'Absolutely, we must go forth for all of man and see what we can learn Penny.' said Ian with a high pitch in his voice.

'It just looks so dark.' said Penny.

'We should not need to worry about the light as the plants in our helmet will light the way.' said Ian.

'And we also have the extra plant leaves that we can use in our hand if needs be.' said Gilbert.

'We should have created lanterns, put the plants in glass spheres and use them to light our way.'

'Quite. If only you had thought of it when we were back on Earth.' said Professor James. 'Who wants to take the lead?'

'I think the honour should be yours this time Professor James.' said Ian.

'If you insist I shall venture forth Ian. But you were robbed of the first honour?'

'Jim, I am an old drunk and I am not sure it would be wise for me to lead us into a dark cave.'

Professor James sniggered and remembered Ian often used to make him laugh down the pub when they were up at Oxford together.

'I suggest that we all walk a few steps behind each other so that if calamity strikes we will not all be caught up in it.'

'Sounds wise to me.' said Giles.

Professor James stepped forward into the darkness.

IX Ghost Planet

The soil dust quickly gave way to strange bronze coloured rock and the light from the plants in his helmet lit the way ahead. Professor James pulled out the large extra leaf he had in the pocket of his flight suit and held it out. He was pleased to watch it glow furiously.

He walked slowly forward, suspecting at any minute he may come across some great chasm and could hear his compatriots marching behind him in single file. They walked for about ten minutes to the back of the cave where it narrowed into a smaller tunnel as if the wind was boring through the rock and this was the point of its focus.

Professor James turned to check that everyone behind him was safe. He could the feel the fresh oxygen from the plants in his suit and also noted to himself that his body temperature was perfect, almost as if they had some futuristic suit that could somehow adjust the temperature. He wondered whether ever such a thing would be possible.

The path started to descend rather sharply and Professor James suggested that they all steady themselves against the wall as they lowered themselves down otherwise one person falling could take the whole group with them. He briefly had a thought of them all sliding down the hill and a smirk crossed his face but he put such childish thoughts out of his head and continued on looking out for any signs of danger.

The eerie silence smashed through their skulls like sudden thunder on a still night. Professor James steadied his breathing and concentrated all he could, perhaps there was really nothing there, perhaps this planet was isolated and desolate yet despite his misgivings he could not escape the feeling that they were not alone. Something was waiting for them like one of the deep-sea fish that he had recently read about that have a bio luminescent light that attracts unwary travellers to a huge mouth of razor-sharp teeth. He felt on his hip for his revolver and was reassured that it was still there.

The party continued on in silence listening out for any sign of life or danger, the dark tunnel continued and they noticed that they still felt no wear in themselves despite the fact they had now been marching for over an hour deep into the bowels of Mars.

Suddenly Professor James threw up his hand and the party stopped.

'Look at these marks on the walls; that is no feat of nature.'

'I fear you are right old man.' said Giles.

'What could have made them' asked Ian.

'I have no idea but they do not appear to be mathematical.' said Gilbert.

'Can we be sure that they are not some kind of erosion formation?' said Dennis.

'Hardly.' replied Giles.

'They look historic to me.' said Ian.

'Is that a horse?' said Penny pointing to one of the patterns.

'Yes, it does look a little like a horse doesn't it.' said Professor James going to rub his chin and then remembering he was wearing a helmet.

'Could there be a civilisation akin to man on Mars.' said Dennis.

'Doubtful.' added Gilbert.

'Perhaps it is man.' said Giles. 'After all, we are here aren't we?'

'That is true but still it is hard to lend that theory credence.' said Ian.

'I think that whatever made those markings was some form of intelligent life.' said Penny.

'Quite.' said Professor James walking forward and turned to ensure that Penny retained her place in the middle of the pack as her safety was his utmost priority.

With renewed uncertainty the expeditioners walked forward like a lone goat in to a forest of wolves. Professor James felt his heart race at the prospect of encountering extra-terrestrial life, he had lived to see so much already on his adventures and the things he had encountered were beyond any schoolboy's dreams but to step foot on another planet, to discover there was other life in another universe, had anyone dared to dream that?

He decided that they would use stealth rather than go blundering in. There were no more markings on the wall and he wished that he could remove his helmet to allow his senses to work a little better, the thick plant lined suits were certainly impairing his hearing and of course he could not smell anything as it was pure air that the plants were exuding.

As he was thinking these thoughts something occurred to him and he held up his hand. There was a faint noise; he was certain of it. The party stopped behind him and he strained his ears, he seriously contemplated removing his helmet for a couple of seconds but decided against it, in case the atmosphere boiled his insides and he spewed out his internal organs or he could not put the helmet back on. He told the others to listen but they could not hear anything. Professor James walked forward but this time a little quicker as he was eager to bring the noise closer to his ears. After a couple of minutes he stopped again.

'It's water.' cried Dennis.

'Or something akin to.' added Ian.

'I suspect we may be close to life.' said Giles.

Professor James said nothing just held up his finger to his face plate to motion for silence and then walked forward, the sound of water growing ever more distinct until it grew into a mighty roar. They walked around a corner and Professor James held up his hand violently, right before them was a great chasm with a huge waterfall chucking out what he guessed to be half a million gallons of water a minute.

They were on a big ledge that spread out and ran alongside the chasm giving them some room, the chasm was extensively deep.

'Look how thick the volume of water is I think that there is more than one source meeting at this point.' said Dennis.

'You mean like many tributaries converging on one point.' said Giles.

'That is exactly what I mean.' said Dennis.

'Just like the Amazon.' said Penny.

'Well done. I shall take you there one day.' said Professor James smiling.

'The mathematics holds it is unlikely that all that water is coming from a single source.'

'Not necessarily Gilbert, it could be a particularly wide river being forced through a single point.' said Ian.

'I can't see any life.' said Dennis.

'No, that's what I was looking for but we probably would not see it on Earth either given how fast the water is moving.' said Professor James.

'Look over there Penny. Down the valley.' said Dennis.

The chasm was of equal height on both sides but only for a short while. The far side dropped down and onto a plain in the distance. In the corner of this plane was another cave and it had some kind of light emitting from it.

'Confound it we have come this far only to be taunted right at the end.' said Giles slapping the wall.

'We must find a way across.'

'But how?' cried Ian.

'We have ropes.' said Giles. 'Perhaps we could try and lasso that rock on the other side and then tie it to the rock on this side.'

'The chasm is too wide you will never get the angle and the distance to cover the rock.' said Gilbert.

'Can we not build a bridge.' said Ian.

'There is nothing to build a bridge out of.' said Penny.

'That is not accurate Penny look at the huge rock on the ledge. Erosion has eroded its base and it is in danger of toppling, if my guesses are accurate and we can persuade it to fall in the right direction, it should cover the ledge.' said Professor James.

'Could one of us not jump into the water with a rope tied to us and then climb up the other side?'

'Dennis that would be highly impractical for a number of reasons. First of all, the rocks on the other side of the chasm look pretty tough to climb. Second, the current is moving so fast you would probably be quickly overwhelmed and drown as the rope meant to save you would effectively hold you under the water. And third the chasm is so deep we may not have enough rope.' said Giles.

'And who said it is water? Maybe it is acid or something.' said Penny.

'The last point scares me the most.' said Dennis looking at Penny.

'What tools do we have with us?' asked Professor James.

'Two pickaxes, a couple of hammers and chisels, some rope, a couple of small saws and some hooks.'

'Thank you Giles. Do you think we could move that rock and cause it to fall over?'

'With some graft maybe.'

'We have two choices we can either return to the ship for some rest and food or we can try and move this rock and it make take several hours.'

'We have plenty of food with us.' said Dennis.

'How are we supposed to eat it in these suits?' asked Penny.

'Confound it.' said Gilbert. 'And how are we supposed to toilet?'

'How is everyone doing in those departments?'

'Well I could do with some food.' said Giles.

The others all agreed.

'And the toilet?' said Ian.

'I could go but can hold it.' said Dennis.

'Me too.' said Gilbert.

'Then let me suggest that we work on this rock and if we can get it done then we will head down to the strange light, have a quick skirmish and then return to the ship and stay in for the next twelve hours or so we can eat plenty, toilet and sleep. Then we will return to explore in earnest. We make this decision as a team, we will either all stay here or we will all return with no exceptions.'

'Let's stay.' said Penny.

'It is not a question in my mind.' said Professor James.

'Absolutely.' added Giles with a pickaxe already in his hand which brought a smile to Professor James' face.

The others all nodded their agreement. Giles and Professor James started at work on the base of the rock with the pickaxes, they had already tried to push it over but even with all of them trying at once there was not even a slight movement. They swung their axes as hard as they could and got into a good rhythm, both the men were alarmed at how much energy they still had in their arms, they did not even tire. They were becoming more and more aware of this plant's supernatural or extra-terrestrial properties. They stopped after about twenty minutes.

'We have barely dented it.' said Giles.

'We should try and move around it, if we chip at it from all sides the whole base should weaken faster.' said Professor James.

'Let me take over?' said Dennis.

'Help yourself.' said Giles handing over the pickaxe.

'I shall take the other one.' said Gilbert.

The hammering continued and the rest of the party sat around the rock chatting as Gilbert and Dennis hammered into the base. They had to speak loud due to the waterfall as well as the continual sound of pickaxes. Professor James carefully monitored progress and was dismayed by what he saw, the rock was exceedingly tough for albeit it was only on a relatively small pivot it was still proving difficult to get through.

Penny was bored as she usually chatted with Dennis in these situations, she started searching her pockets and came across her gun, she nearly pulled it out to have a couple of shots but thought better of it as her uncle would not be pleased. She came across her spare leaf that they all carried but there was something else at the bottom of her pocket. It felt hard and small. Penny pulled it out to inspect it.

'Uncle James, I have an idea, look what I found in my pocket. I am ashamed to say that I stole it from Ian's desk when we first arrived and have carried it as a kind of lucky charm ever since. Can we not use it to bring the colossal rock down somehow.'

'A piece of the meteorite; that is useful. If we could create an electrical current and ignite it we may be able to use it to go through the base at the bottom, it is so tough that the rock will have no choice but to give way.' said Professor James.

'I think I can help you there.'

'How so Ian?' said Giles.

'I knew that we needed an electric current to provide electricity and as you all know we used a dynamo to start the Mad Professor. It occurred to me that wherever we are we should have that valuable resource to hand and be in a position to use it. Hence in my bag I have some milk, some meteorite and a portable dynamo.'

'You jest?' said Professor James.

'I do not. Here it is.' said he pulling out a small metal box with a handle on it.

'Ian you astound me sometimes.' said Giles.

'And me.' said Gilbert who had stopped hammering.

'It is just logic Giles and a mind for practicality as you would appreciate.'

'Indeed I do Ian, when sailing the oceans you have to be prepared for anything which is why I am so impressed, you are welcome to come exploring with me anytime.'

'Thank you Giles, it nice to be reassured that I am not just a crazy old drunk.'

'Do you think we could ignite that shard of meteorite and fire the propulsion to cut through the rock or at least weaken it?'

'Yes, I cannot see why not.' replied Ian.

'Well done Penny.' said Professor James with a huge smile.

'You did not bring me along because of my looks uncle.'

'No, he brought you along because he was blackmailed.' said Giles.

The party erupted in laughter but Penny did not even smile.

'Well let us get on with it then.' said she.

'Perhaps we should try and create an indent for the shard to go into.' said Dennis.

'Excellent idea, if you two both hammer at the same point in the rock, we can insert the meteorite shard into the hole.' said Ian.

'Let us take over again.' said Giles.

Professor James and Giles took over and were soon working in unison. The others remarked that they looked like some sort of automated machinery. Giles and the Professor worked tirelessly for about ten minutes and when they eventually pulled back there was small hole in the rock.

Professor James was more than aware of the amount of physical exertion he had committed to thus far yet he still felt nothing, he wondered whether when they returned to Earth and no longer needed the plants if he would even be able to move his body. Would it just seize up or would he fall into a coma from exhaustion? It was not an immediate problem but he made a mental note to talk it through with the others later on.

'Ian you can take over now.' said he.

Penny handed over the shard of meteorite and Professor James placed it in the nook that they had created. He told everyone to stand back and then wound the device with the handle, put the two connectors on the crystal and pressed a button, the meteorite ignited with such force that Ian leapt back, they saw it starting to shake the rock, the energy was intense and they could hear the sound of it trying to bore through the rock but there could only be one victor. It was not long before a crack appeared in the base of the rock and they all cheered, Giles did so with his salutary Hurrah!

There was an almighty cracking noise as the whole base of the rock fissured.

'*Now.*' screamed Professor James.

Following his lead they ran and pushed the rock as hard they could, they heard it cracking and crumbling as it gave away and slowly they felt the rock falling out of their hands.

It crashed down with a thud that reverberated throughout the whole cavern. Professor James inspected it, as predicted it had cleared the chasm and landed on the other side. He checked its cracks and fissures but the main body of the rock remained intact and in one solid unified piece.

'I am pretty sure that it is safe to cross, I cannot see any fractures created by the force of landing. What do you think Giles?'

Giles walked around both sides. 'Let me answer your question like this Professor James.' said he jumping up on the rock and running across it.

'Damn fool you are sometimes Giles.' replied he crossing the rock and joining Giles on the other side. The others all walked across with a little more caution.

'Let's continue single file and maintain silence.'

'What an extraordinary thing to say. It is a little late for that don't you think Professor James?' said Ian.

'I am aware that we have just made an awful lot of noise but we are also by a raging torrent of water which is making just as much noise. I am the expedition leader and say we maintain silence because if anything other than us makes a noise I need to be able to hear it.'

'Pulling rank at last are we Professor.' said Giles.

'Shut it Giles this is not time for your tomfoolery.'

'Just an observation is all.' said Ian rolling his eyes.

'Let us get going I am as hungry as I am excited.' said Penny.

'Me too.' said Dennis.

They trudged along the ravine until they came to the edge and saw a rough jagged descent to the plateau below.

'We will have to climb down. Do you think you can all manage it?' said Professor James.

'The climb is not hard and the gradient is not that steep, the rocks are almost forming a staircase.' said Gilbert.

'Should not be a problem, in fact, we can probably get down there quite quickly.'

'It is not a race Dennis if one of us falls and breaks their leg, it is going to be very difficult to get them home.'

'I know that Gilbert but it should still be a fast descent.'

'Let us not forget that we also have to get back up.' said Penny.

'I think we should be alright but we have come too far to stop now in any case. Do not underestimate, we know nothing of what to expect and that is always a dangerous thing.'

Professor James led the way again and climbed down on to the top of the first boulder, it was not slippery and found that he had quite a good grip but as he suspected it was not as easy as it looked. You had to carefully step between the rocks and gently lower yourself off the larger ones. As they were wearing their suits it was not as easy to keep a grip with their hands. Professor James warned everyone to be careful not to slip between the jagged cracks, you could easily break several limbs and if you were unfortunate to bounce down some then you were probably doomed.

It was hard work but they were still wide awake. Professor James noted his muscles still did not ache, this was of a growing concern as it was highly unnatural, he should be feeling something by now. The descent continued without incident with the exception of a near slip by every one of them which served as a timely reminder to respect the rockface.

It was Penny who was first to reach the bottom, she lowered herself onto the plateau floor and leapt with excitement.

'I did it.'

'Penny, perhaps a little quiet is in order.' said Professor James joining her.

The rest of the party descended. They gathered themselves and rechecked all their equipment then marched toward the glowing light. They were soon at the entrance to the cave, the hue looked green and purple but it was hard to tell as the plants in their helmet also lit up the way. The cave was filled with a strange fog and they could not see through it.

'Giles you better take the lead with me.' said Professor James pulling out his revolver.

'Yes. We had better be vigilant.'

'Everybody else is to walk fifteen feet behind us and have your weapons to hand. If I fire a shot you are to turn back immediately and return to the plateau.'

'What has you spooked so?'

'Just precaution Ian.' said Professor James marching forward into the fog.

The mist was intense and they trod each step like a child stepping onto a frozen pond, they were unsure of their footing, what if there was a cliff, they would walk straight off. Professor James touched the sides of the cave and realised that they were wet.'

'Looks like condensation.' said Giles.

'That would require humidity?' replied Professor James looking at Giles. He stopped and mopped some up on his glove. 'It looks like water.'

'I think if we are going to encounter any life it will be here.' said Giles.

'That's why I have my gun drawn.'

They continued down the tunnel and followed it as it snaked downwards, it seemed to twist like the path of a sidewinder and they were both at odds to defy how this could have been naturally made. There were no more markings on any of the walls. A large gust of wind came rattling down the tunnel and the fog disappeared revealing that the tunnel exited onto another large ledge.

Giles and Professor James walked forward and looked over the precipice, far below them was a huge valley that went as far as the eye could see in every direction, there were plants and crystals everywhere, they could see movement and spotted creatures flying through the air.

X The Martian Valley

'Professor James I am glad to confirm that there is life on Mars.' said Ian.

Giles and the Professor stood there transfixed watching the strange alien landscape that was beyond anything they could have ever hoped for.

'I wish I brought my spy glass.' said Professor James.

'I did.' said Ian.

Professor James turned to see that the entire party had arrived. Ian gave him the spyglass. Professor James looked through it and saw strange creatures below, none of which he could recognise. 'This is inconceivable whatever these creatures are none of them are known to man.'

'We have discovered extra-terrestrial life Uncle; we will be the greatest scientists in history.' said Penny clapping her hands.

'It is incredible.' said Dennis.

'Beyond my imagination.' said Gilbert taking the spyglass.

They all stood there absorbing the unfamiliar view. Professor James took the telescope and began to look down the ledge.

'It looks like there is a path leading down to it.'

'Let me have a look.' said Giles.

Giles followed the path down to the plateau with his telescope.

'It's a bit too convenient for my liking.'

'I was thinking the same I suspect that the path has been created by the traversing of creatures rather than erosion.

'Perhaps it is an old river bed.'

'You can tell it is not Dennis and besides the water would just cascade over the ledge.' said Giles.

'Are you saying that someone has built a path to lead us down to the plateau?'

'No Penny that it not what I am saying, we are not expected and animals of all varieties and presumably on all planets are curious, my guess is that many a creature over the years have grown curious of what is on the ledge and beyond, there could have been more fertile feeding grounds.'

'Precisely' said Giles.

'Are we all ok to continue?'

The party all agreed and this time there was no mention of food or toilet requirements as such was the excitement of the discovery.

They walked as a group now that they could clearly see ahead, they all relaxed and talked about the journey so far and speculated about what life they would encounter and how intelligent it was. Professor James believed he had already made a wondrous discovery that would delight everyone. He was keeping it to himself until he had confirmed his suspicions. They got to the bottom and were immediately greeted by strange looking trees and plants that writhed and turned.

'Look over there at those plants do they not look familiar to everyone.' said Dennis.

'Good God.' cried Ian, 'They are the plants that we have in our suits. They did come from Mars.'

'That's not all my dear boy, look over there.'

They all followed the direction of Professor James's finger.

'Confound it. The meteorite as well.' said Ian slapping Professor James on the back.

'Look around carefully can anyone *not* see any of our plants anywhere in their view.'

'No.' said Penny. 'They're everywhere.'

'Indeed they are. I have purposefully been looking out across the chasm monitoring them and they are everywhere as far as the eye can see.'

'But how come we did not notice before uncle?'

'Because of the plants in our helmet they have distorted our view via their colouration of our sight. You had no way of telling that they were the same colour as everything looks green though a green filter. I looked at their shape and structure and was convinced, then when I saw the green crystal I knew it must be so.'

'Fascinating.' said Dennis.

'You still do not understand the ramifications of my revelation I see.'

'What do you mean Professor?' said Gilbert.

'It is easier if I show you.' replied he

'*Nooo.*' screamed Penny running forward.

Giles held her back 'He knows what he is doing child.'

Professor James removed his helmet, there was a stunned silence and Professor James had his large spare leaf ready to slam to his mouth and nose. He inhaled deeply.

'You see the air is breathable down here, the plants are pumping out oxygen at an incredible rate and due to the vast quantity of them they have created a macro atmosphere.'

'Are you sure?' said Dennis.

'That is a damned stupid question.' said Gilbert.

'I am not deceased am I?' said Professor James taking off his protective suit.

The rest of the party removed their helmets and breathed in the air which seemed fresher than a summer meadow in June.

After a cacophony of animation there was nothing but a pile of suits left. Professor James stood there and laughed whilst everyone had disappeared to go to the toilet. When the party returned they all dived for their rations. Professor James suggested they sit and rest on the path so that they can eat and replenish their energy. He warned them that albeit they did not feel tired their legs have had quite an exertion and as far as he knew it was possible that they could be doing damage to themselves and not be aware of it.

They sat around and began to eat, Ian had brought a bottle of wine, they shared it around in celebration. He took a nip from his hip flask to keep his alcohol addiction at bay. As they stood and watched Penny remarked that they should make some sketches of what they could see. Feeling refreshed from the food Penny started sketching away.

Professor James pulled out his pipe and filled it as did Giles, they smiled at each other and tapped their pipes as if they were glasses in a pub. Professor James inhaled a gulp of the tobacco and exhaled it slowly, savouring the rich feeling of the smoke pouring out of him like a volcano in the pacific.

'You know this maybe the best smoke I have ever had.'

'I agree.' said Giles as a large flame proclaimed his pipe alive. 'If I was given the choice between food or a smoke, I am not sure I wouldn't have gone for the pipe.'

They sat and lay in a group each one of them really enjoying the moment. They smoked, ate and drank, everyone was in good humour and trying to savour the moment.

'If we do not need the suits, perhaps we should hide them somewhere, then come back and collect them.' said Giles standing up.

'That's a good idea.' said Penny sipping the last of her wine.

'Perhaps under these plants over there. Then we shall know as soon we get to the path where they are.'

'Good idea Dennis. We will certainly need them again let us not forget that if we lose those suits we will be unable to get back to the ship.' said Professor James.

'Mmm.' said Gilbert.

'What bothers you?'

'I am wondering whether we should put all our suits in one place Professor James?'

'We should not have to worry about them being stolen or destroyed, but since all of our lives depend on the suits perhaps we should hide them out of view.'

'I may seem paranoid but I would always be with the side of caution.' said Gilbert.

'Quite right, it has saved me many a time, I remember one time sailing near some islands in the pacific when I got a hunch that all about me was not quite right, I swung the ship as violently as I could out into the open sea and with seconds to spare, for just below the water line was a huge sand bank, we would have been shipwrecked for sure.' said Giles.

'We are a fine team.' said Ian.

'Hurrah.' said Giles.

'Hurrah.' they all cried in unison.

After hiding the suits on either side of the path they got up and headed into the valley. The grass seemed crispy like park land after a heavy frost. There were many worn out tracks obviously made by animals and creatures.

'Look Uncle James over there. Something blue just moved.'

They all crept forward and through the weird shaped leaves and writhing plants, a blue object was slowly moving through it.

'What is it?' asked Penny.

'A stupid question Penny.' said Professor James.

'What you mean you have not got your encyclopaedia of wildlife on Mars with you?'

'Giles, why you aren't in theatre I will never understand.'

'Oh no, annoying you is too much fun.'

'Quite.' replied Professor James.

Giles looked at Penny and winked at her.

'It looks to like some kind of Martian horse.' said Ian.

'Its features are so bizarre.' added Gilbert.

'It looks like it could be amphibious.' said Dennis scratching his ginger stubble.

Professor James studied it intensely, it was the size of small horse and walked on all fours, it was a metallic dark blue in colour and had no tail. Its eyes were large and black facing forward like that of man. Its feet were odd, the front set were like a set of large sausages curling and meeting the ground flat, whilst the rear legs were spindlier and had talons on them. Above its mouth were three bulbous strips of flesh that hung down like a strip door.

'They look docile.' said Penny.

'It has seen us.' said Gilbert.

The strange creature inspected them with its beady black eyes and then continued on as before.

'I think we should be safe from them.' said Giles.

'I concur,' said Professor James.

They approached the animal but it moved away.

'Let us not interfere with it, perhaps when it gets used to us, it will allow us to get close.' said Giles.

'Agreed.' said Professor James.

'Look there are more blue horses.' cried Penny walking over to another one, it hesitated, then quickly walked off.

'They act more like cows than horses to me.' said Dennis.

'What an interesting observation.' said Ian.

'They intrigue me. I think we should do a field study on them once we have sated our exploratory appetite.' said Dennis.

'Indeed but I fear that maybe a long time.' said Giles.

'We should do a comprehensive field study of everything here.'

'We cannot stay here forever Penny, we only have supplies for so long and we must give ourselves ample time to return home, we need to cover ourselves in case of something going awry.' replied Professor James.

'What can go wrong?' said Gilbert.

'You're incredulous man. What if we get back to the Mad Professor, it will not start and we have just one meal left, it may take us a week to get it going by which we will die from starvation.' said Professor James unclenching his fist and pulling out a cigarette.

'Professor James is right, I knew someone who was exploring an uncharted island once, he went ashore for a few nights camping but only took a small amount of food knowing that he could row back to the ship to restock. That night a tropical storm blew in, wrecked the ship and killed most on board, he was then forced to live off the island for a few months which took some skill and a lot of patience.'

'Did he survive?' asked Penny.

'Yes he did. You are looking at him.' said Giles with a warm smile.

Professor James laughed.

They walked further into the hidden kingdom amongst the familiar oxygen breathing plants and the green meteorite. The temperature was warm and slightly humid but manageable. Professor James noted to himself that it was out of synch, the humidity he felt was not in alignment with the temperature of the air, this microclimate had rules of its own and he wondered how physics applied to Mars or its Martian bowels. They saw strange insects and a one-legged frog that sat on a huge leg and jumped incredibly high and far. They decided to name them Cyclops frogs despite the fact that they had two eyes that looked remarkably similar to frog eyes on Earth.

'In the land of the crippled the one-legged frog is king.' quipped Penny which made everybody laugh.

The blue horses were still in abundance and there were also now pink jelly creatures that scuffled along and seemed to be akin to a slug yet they were the size of a small dog, they tried to examine one and was astounded that that they could not find any mouth eyes or legs, it was just a pink mass. They considered that perhaps it was some kind of land borne jelly fish. Penny quickly sketched one before they moved on.

'Look, a purple meteorite.' shouted Ian.

They walked over to the large chunk sticking out of the ground.

'It seems to be of the same quality.' said Giles.

'We must get a sample.' said Ian.

Before anyone could say a word Ian took the pickaxe off Giles and brought it down as hard as he could.

'Blimey, nearly broke my arm it is as strong as the green stuff.'

'Here let me.' said Giles swinging with all his might. 'Yes, definitely not going to break.'

'You don't learn do you.' said Professor James.

'Ian, where is the milk?'

'Why yes of course Penny. I do not know what condition it is in mind?'

Ian pulled a small bottle out of his back pack and poured some of the milk on a piece sticking out on its own.

'Nothing. It has not softened it or anything.' said Ian.

'Perhaps because it has gone off.' said Dennis.

'No that is not so, I am pretty confident it is the calcium that it reacts to.' replied Ian.

'We have plenty of time; let us return to it later.' said Gilbert.

'Where has Professor James gone?' said Giles.

'He is over there.' said Dennis. 'He is examining something.'

The all moved over to where Professor James was standing. He had his hands on his hips and was deep in thought.

'What on Earth is it?' asked Penny. 'Why do you look so concerned?'

'Look at these Martian fruit or vegetables.'

'They look like a cross between a strawberry and aubergine but yellow.' said Gilbert.

'You are not seeing, forget what they look like, what is wrong with this picture?'

The party remained silent for a moment.

'They are alien.'

'Martian, rather.' said Gilbert throwing Dennis a look.

'By Jove.' said Giles walking forward and kneeling down at the first plant. 'These have been planted, they are in vertical rows and each plant is exactly the same distance apart.' Giles took some rope and measured, he looked up at the expedition.

'Without a long rule I could not be certain but I would say that these are a barely a millimeter out of equidistance from each other.'

'And the question that bothers me is who or what planted them?' said Professor James.

'Is it not possible that this species of plant grows like this? We cannot apply the rules of Earth to Mars can we.' said Ian.

'No we cannot, you are quite right there, but I still find it highly unlikely.' said Professor James looking in every direction to see if they were being watched.

'As a botanist I concur with Professor James, Ian. There must be some biology in it even if they are Martian and I find it almost inconceivable that they would grow the exact distance apart?'

'Just trying to think things from all angles that is all.'

'When you bring in to the equation the markings on the wall it is too much of a coincidence, there is intelligent life about and they probably know we are here. Since we do not know what we are dealing with let us show respect, do not willfully destroy anything or set about making trouble out of boredom.' said Professor James.

'We are scientist's not a gang of recidivist ruffians.' said Gilbert. 'Why would we do such things?'

'I obviously exaggerate but let us keep in mind that in all likelihood we are in someone or something's garden.'

'Extraordinary.' said Giles.

'Do you think we could eat one?' said Penny.

'Not worth the risk but we can collect one on our way back through.' said Ian.

They purposefully walked around the edge and saw more fields full of various Martian produce all of which was unrecognisable to the scientific eye. Professor James feasted on the abundance of new discoveries before them and thought they should try and bring teams of scientists to do a huge field study, the potential for their increase in knowledge was unfathomable and perhaps they had been thinking about the universe in completely the wrong way.

They were now walking through long black grass that moved out of their way as they approached. Professor James could not relax as his primary objective now was to find the intelligent life on Mars.

After ten or so minutes the grass yielded and they found themselves walking on rubbery weeds. The sound of water filled their ears and they saw a large river ahead of them.

'A river. There really is a complete ecosystem down here.' remarked Gilbert.

'Quite.' said Professor James.

'I wonder if it is water as we know it?'

'I doubt it Ian; it is purple.' said Giles.

'Yes, but it could be soil or all manner of things that are causing it. The Thames is brown isn't it?'

'Dennis has a point.' said Penny walking over and looking into the river.

'Is there life in the river?' said Giles.

'I would think yes after all the life we have seen.' said Ian.

'Look there are weird hippo pig things at the water's edge.'

Professor James looked up and could see a pack of stumpy creatures with chubby legs drinking, they had two thick snouts that protruded out and they were using them to suck up the water, one of them drank with one and lifted the other in the air and Professor James guessed that it must have a sense of smell. One of the creatures stuck both of its snouts in the air and as he did the other five or six followed suit, they all ran off across the field.

'What is their problem?' said Penny shoving her sketch pad violently back into her bag.

'Don't know but think I just saw something move in the water.' said Dennis.

XI The Thing

'Where?' said Penny.

'Over there. It looked like a large fish.'

Professor James looked at the small herd of pig creatures that had ran off as fast as their stumpy legs could move, he quickly realised there must have been a reason why they had ran, he assumed they had detected their presence but another thought occurred as they had been drinking at the water's edge.

'*Penny away from the water now!*' shouted Professor James.

A huge grey tentacle came out of the water, Penny screamed and dived to the floor as it swung past her head. Another one came out, grabbed her and Penny went flying into the air, before anyone could react there was a gunshot as Professor James let off some shots at the creature's body.

'It looks like some kind of giant cephalopod.' cried Giles.

Penny landed on the bank violently and rolled as soon as she landed. The animal seemed enraged and another tentacle came up and grabbed Dennis.

Dennis managed to pull out his gun and fired but another tentacle rose up and knocked it out of his hand. They all joined in shooting at the fleshy bulb but the bullets seemed only to enrage it further. It came closer and a huge tentacle swept along the bank and knocked both Giles and Ian flying. Giles got it worst as he was struck straight across the chest and flew a considerable distance. Professor James emptied a round of bullets into the beast. He could see Dennis being swung about in the air and then slammed violently into the water.

'It's a Kraken.' cried Penny.

Ian and Professor Gilbert opened fire.

Giles was back on his feet and running at it firing his gun as well.

'Aim for the tentacle that has Dennis. All of us at once.' said Professor James.

'Penny already had her gun up and fired three shots consecutively. All three hit their desired target and Dennis fell into the water right next to the bank, he quickly pulled himself up. As he did Professor James took a run at it firing straight at the front of its fleshy mound. Giles ran and grabbed Dennis.

'*Run, run away from the river, cephalopods cannot leave water.*' cried Giles.

Professor James ducked as a tentacle swipe just missed him, then he had to dive again as another tentacle the size of a small tree trunk thudded down in front of him. They ran but the tentacles kept coming, they looked back and to their horror saw the creature walk on land with four giant legs, it had tusks like a mammoth and a huge squid like body on top, it also had a quivering curtain at the front near the tusks and when it lifted there were sets of black eyes and sharp spiked teeth.

Penny was caught again and so was Dennis, it had run after them with considerable ease and they could all feel the reverberations in the ground as it ran. Now it had Penny, Professor James felt his blood boil and rage misted over him.

'*My niece. You dare to attack my niece.*' he turned to fire this time aiming at its face. Ian followed suit as did Gilbert but its face veil protected it.

'Giles, pass the machete.' said Professor James.

'Catch.' said Giles.

Ian took cover behind a tree as did Gilbert. Giles looked at Professor James with concern in his eyes. They were trapped and the only way to escape was to abandon Penny and Dennis and that was something that no one was prepared to do.

Professor James just stood there looking at the creature that was trying to eat Penny and Dennis. Every time it brought them toward its mouth Gilbert, Ian and Giles let off a volley of shots.

Professor James tightened his mouth and pulled out his knife so he was holding the dagger and the machete in either hand. He walked slowly toward the giant creature. One of the huge tentacles quickly swooped down and grabbed him, he could feel its wet slimy grip was very powerful and could probably crush him to death.

'Penny, hold on, I will get you out.'

'Uncle James what the hell are you doing?'

'Professor are you mad we will all get eaten.' said Dennis punching the arm that had him.

'No we won't.'

The quadruped cephalopod threw Professor James around like he was in a tornado but it did not phase Professor James as that is what he wanted, he was swung over the water and nearly collided with Penny and Dennis, then he was back over the land and finally it brought him up over its own body. Professor James used his dagger and stabbed the tentacle, as intended it let him go and he fell onto the body, he timed it perfectly, letting the machete fall like a spear he drove it straight into the front of the curtain that protected its face guessing that that was where the brain was. Dark green blood spurted out. The creature let out a terrific wail and lifted the curtain to scream, it was met by a hail of bullets from Giles, Gilbert and Ian that all hit the target smashing through the face and into the brain.

Professor James used the dagger to stab it again but this time to pull himself up as he did not want to fall in front of its mouth. The amount of blood was terrific but as the animal was so large it did not mean it was dead, the Professor pulled himself up with the dagger and then using all his might pulled out the machete and used it to hoist himself further up. The creature crashed to the ground face forward, Professor James pulled both weapons out of the skin, slid down to the ground rolled, got up and ran over to Penny.

In a final act of defiance the huge kraken like creature had thrown Penny and Dennis through the air. They had both been thrown with considerable force and high through the air, this creature was determined not to be the only casualty that day.

'Penny, my dear Penny are you alright?'

'It hurts Uncle James.'

'What hurts darling?'

'Everything. My arms, legs, I landed with such force.'

'Can you move?'

'Yes.'

'I want you to slowly roll on to your back.'

Penny did as instructed, Professor James could see some scrapes and grazes but nothing disastrous.

'Very slowly I want you to move all of your limbs one by one.'

'Bend your arms and raise them, then do the same with your legs, if the pain is too much stop.'

Again Penny followed instruction. 'Yes, I can move everything.'

'I think you are ok, you are probably just badly bruised and will likely start feel very stiff for the next few days.'

'That's ok the nearest hospital is only a hundred million miles away.'

'A hundred and forty actually.' said Giles leaning down and examining her. 'It looks like bruising to me as well.'

They helped her to her feet, she tried to walk and found that she had a bad limp.

'I just need a few minutes of walking on it and then it will become good enough to walk on.' said Penny leaning on her uncle's shoulder for support.

'Where is Gilbert and Ian?'

'They are checking on Dennis.'

Professor James looked up and saw Ian swigging heavily from his hip flask and Gilbert was on his knees.

'Oh no.'

'What is it uncle?'

'I fear it is bad news look where he landed.'

'Blast, he had the misfortune of landing on the meteorite, that would be like landing on spears of glass.'

Professor James held up his niece and they started to walkover. He told Penny to prepare herself in case it was not good.

As they got close Gilbert approached them with bloodshot eyes. 'Dennis is no longer with us.'

'Confound that damned creature.' said Professor James. He walked over and saw red blood running over green diamond that created a macabre and interesting pattern of death. Then he saw Dennis' face on one of the jagged edges that had gone through the back of his skull but it looked like his body had been punctured many times. His eyes were open as was his mouth as if he was trying to say his last words.

Gilbert got up and pulled Dennis' eyelids shut with his fingers and placed two coins on his eyes. Before anyone could ask he turned and said,

'He made me promise, he did not really believe in the boatman and the River Styx but he liked the idea of it.'

'Well good journey my friend.' said Giles.

'Here is to your greatest field trip yet.' said Ian raising his hip flask.

Penny burst out in an uncontrollable sob.

They stood there looking at the bloodied corpse somehow in disbelief, whenever you set out for adventure you are always aware of the multitudes of danger that pursue you like a rabid dog yet when you eventually get bitten it still comes as a surprise.

Professor James fought hard to control his emotions and found himself welling up, it was he that brought Dennis into the adventure. Professor James briefly remembered his father who scalded him for crying in public when his grandfather had died, 'be a man and master your emotions,' he had told him.

Professor James turned and saw Penny crying in Giles' arms, he went over to her and she immediately embraced him, he could feel her hot breath and his shirt wetting from her tears.

'Now then Penny it is terrifically tragic what we have borne witness to today but Dennis was one of the first men to Mars, he has seen what no one else on Earth has seen and maybe never will. I am sure he would prefer to be living but I can assure you if he had the choice to be still living or to be dead but having visited Mars I know what he would have chosen. To be sincere with you I think that is what you would choose as well. I certainly would.' said Professor James.

'I .. I ... I guess your right but it's just so sad. I am going to miss him terribly so'

'You are right Penny and we will mourn him but remember what I have told you sometimes you have to be a monster so to speak. We are one hundred and forty million miles from home and we still do not know what awaits us. So as much as I want to grieve and stop all that I am doing, I cannot as I still have five lives to think of.'

'I'm sorry uncle.'

Professor James gently pushed her away wiped his niece's hair away from her eyes and took her chin. 'Don't ever be sorry, the emotions you are showing are natural but if you are to be an effective scientist and adventurer you must learn to master them. You can see that Giles has tears in his eyes don't you?'

'Yes.'

'You listen to our next conversation it will be pragmatic. Behind closed doors when he is back at his desk with a bottle of rum, his pipe and a guarantee that no one will see and hear him, he will cry as much as you I should think. Now compose yourself and sit on the grass while we discuss how this impacts things.'

'I'm sorry I never envisaged that it would lead to one us being deceased.'

'It is not your fault we are all adventurers, we know what we are in for, albeit I will confess I did not see it coming like this.'

'So what do we do know?' asked Gilbert with silent tears running down his face.

'We bury him.' said Professor James.

'Can we not take him back?' replied Gilbert.

'No, he has to be buried here,'

'Dennis was my understudy, he will go back home and be buried by his family.'

'No Gilbert he will not. It will use all our strength to carry him and also as he is now a corpse and we don't know how long we will be in the spaceship for, a decomposing body is not an ideal travelling companion is it?'

'Steady on Professor.' said Giles gently grabbing his arm.

'Now you know why I don't like being the bloody leader.' said Professor James lighting a cigarette.

'It makes sense Gilbert, we will bury him and say a few prayers.' said Ian looking at the body.

'Check his body and back pack take his rations and supplies we may need them.'

Ian and Gilbert looked up at Giles.

'Do not look at Giles like that, he is right, we are devasted by this event but we need to think logically if we are to survive and look at the amount of ammo we just used on that one encounter, we need every bullet we can get.'

'It is a shame he discarded his back pack it may have saved his life.' said Penny.

'Hindsight is a luxury that no one can possess so it is not worthy of thought. We all discarded our bags to give manoeuvrability to the fight.' said Ian.

'I didn't.' said Giles 'and have a bloody sore back because of it.'

'Can we get on with the burial please?' said Gilbert.

They removed Dennis from the stones; his red hair was matted with blood. They took his supplies and divided it amongst themselves. It took them forty-five minutes of solid graft to dig a deep enough hole. They remained in silence, most of them chain smoking and Ian had a few more trips than usual to his flask. They lowered Dennis into the ground and albeit they were forced to drop him in, they did so as slowly as they could. Gilbert jumped into the grave to put the coins back on his eyes.

They all said a few words and a small prayer but Penny was by far the most gracious and went on for several minutes giving him a glowing report of both his personal and professional life and then she finished with a heart-felt prayer.

Afterwards they all agreed they should have just let Penny doing the talking. Penny wrote his name and the year of his birth and death on a piece of paper and stuck it on the shallow mound.

'Should we continue much further?' said Gilbert.

'Yes, look at all we have discovered so far?' said Giles.

'But one of us has perished?' said he.

'People perish all the time, do you know how many shipwrecks I have been in, we do not give up or cower at the first hint of tragedy, we are scientific explorers this is what we do.'

'I empathise with your gusto but I am just trying to be rational and to me it seems pointless now.'

'You're grieving old man and I fully understand, I think you may still be in shock. This was no more than a tragic accident if it were not for the rocks he would still be here and from that viewpoint I think we should carry on forward.'

'Gilbert, apologies for my shortness with you earlier. It is a tough time for us all.'

'Not at all Professor. I understand. I just can't believe he's gone.'

'Allow me to ask you something. What would he want us to do?'

'You have me there.' said Gilbert swigging his beer. 'He would have wanted us to carry on.'

'The purpose of this mission was to reach Mars, then once we had succeeded it became to investigate the cave and now we have discovered a hidden world and are unlocking its secrets. I think we must have boundaries but the climax of this voyage is the discovery of the intelligent life on this planet, what made those markings and what planted the vegetables?'

'You are right Professor James we must honour him by completing the expedition.' said Gilbert.

The others looked at each other and all nodded but remained silent.

'What has happened is terrible and I to want grieve as much as you all, the death of Dennis is weighing heavy on my conscience but we are in the field and this is all the time we have to grieve. We are lucky we have had that. It is very difficult but we must try and pause our grief, once we are back home then we will grieve properly and hold a full memorial but right now we have a job to do and five other lives are at stake, including your own.'

They walked in silence each one deep in their thoughts. Professor James led without question and purposefully strode ahead to get some space. He thought about Dennis and how he was now another face in a hallway of tragedy that seemed to follow him and his adventures. As always he questioned why he put himself in this position, he knew the reason and the cause of science was a just one as far as he was concerned. He half-heartedly vowed never to go on an expedition again but as he finished the sentence in his head he knew it to be untrue. He hated the mantle of leadership that was always thrust upon him and he now felt personally responsible for Dennis' death.

He thought of Penny and cursed under his breath, he remonstrated that she was an adult now and if she was to live to the full and be a scientist in her own right then who was he to stand in the way of that? He made a silent prayer that he would live to see that day and that he would be mercifully slain before he saw the day that she herself perished.

Professor James looked ahead using the telescope and in the distance he saw there was a tributary of the river that split off into a canyon.

Professor James gathered the group and they all took it in turns looking through one by one. This find was just what the group needed and they decided to name the place Dennis Canyon. They marched on and saw more of the weird pig creatures and the blue horses as well as some weird six-legged creature that moved exceedingly fast and looked akin to a beetle except there were no horns or tusks. Penny tried to catch one but she was too slow.

As they neared the canyon they saw their first flying creature of a decent size. It looked about the size of an eagle but had teeth like a shark and a furry head yet its body was scaly and its mighty wings were membrane like that of bats. It swooped without warning and plucked something out of the river, they saw another one give chase, wanting to share in the spoils.

The abundance of life increased, animals were burying themselves into the ground, flying through the sky and disturbing the water. As scientists they knew there was enough work to last a decade and as they walked they realised that the only way to do an effective field study would be to colonise it.

It had not escaped their attention that Dennis was fine after coming out of the water so it was not acid or harmful in the first instance but that did not mean that it was safe to drink and no one had noticed whether he spat any out of his mouth. They checked their drinks supply which for the time being was acceptable.

It was an hour before they got close to the canyon. Professor James made his way to see where the river split in case there was anything to be gained by looking at the junction.

'It looks perfectly normal to me.' said Giles.

'Yes, I was hoping it may be man ... Martian made.' said Professor James.

'Crossing this river is going to be a problem.' said Gilbert.

'I just thought that but it is the canyon we are interested in for the moment.' said Ian.

Professor James looked as the river flowed straight ahead on either side, it was meadows and trees but to their left the grassland hit the wall of the cavern, where the river had carved a canyon through the side of it.

As the party continued in, Professor James and Giles took the opportunity to have a quiet smoke together.

'How are you faring old man?'

'I am fine thanks Giles, there is nothing one can do but continue on, you know that.'

'Yes I know. We have lost too many now. Exploration is a dangerous business.'

'What possesses us to seek out such things Giles?'

'It is who we are.'

'It is who you are. I am quite at home in a lab.'

'Your home is with scientific discovery with me.'

'Maybe it is as you say, I just worry about Penny, I promised my brother nothing would ever happen to her.'

'You cannot worry about such things. Imagine someone refrained you from being a scientist, she is her own person and has studied hard, now you must let her tread her own path. It is only natural to worry about her, I do as well, I have known her since she was a little girl don't forget.'

'I know Giles apologies, you are just about as much an uncle to her as I am.'

'Listen James.'

Professor James turned his head to look at Giles as he rarely called him by Christian name.

'We are on Mars, the very first expedition in the history of mankind and Penny is one of us, no matter what happens, her place in history is guaranteed and that has got to be worth the risk. It certainly is from her point of view.'

'Quite.' said Professor James taking a heavy pull on his cigarette. 'What is that up there Giles? Does that look like a trail leading up to that ledge to you?'

XII The Quarrelsome Canyon

'It certainly does. Let us check out the canyon from the bottom and see if we can find the start of the trail.'

'That seems like a grand idea.'

They continued walking on without informing the rest of the party that had started to catch up to them. They arrived at the canyon and were wary as they had to go to the water's edge.

'Good God, look, they look like dwellings?' cried Gilbert.

'Dwellings? It looks like Petra, look at the pillars and the square windows, the triangular openings are a little odd though.' said Giles.

'What could have created that?' said Penny.

'That would be the intelligent life that has been evading us our entire journey.'

'Do you think that they know that we are here Professor James?' said Ian.

'I do and further to that I am sure that there is something that we have missed.'

'Elaborate.' said Penny.

'I don't know Penny but I have the feeling that we are being watched and that they have monitored our progress the whole time. I have a real unease in this place, beautiful as it is and foregoing the more dangerous of the local wildlife of course.'

'Strange that I have not had the same experience.'

'Giles, deep down you are always a little giddy when we find somewhere new. You should be careful it sometimes throws you off.'

'It has served me well so far.'

'It was an observation not a slight.' replied Professor James.

'This is amazing. I think they have built a city.' said Ian.

They stood there mesmerised by the bright bronze coloured buildings that had been carved out of rock.

'Well that puts paid to that?' said Gilbert inspecting his facial growth in a pocket mirror and then combing his hair for good measure.

'What?' said Professor James.

'To the question of whether there is intelligent life on Mars.' replied he.

'Yes quite. I think we should use that path as an observation deck to see if we can observe what we are dealing with. We have no assurance that our trespass will be welcome.'

'They will probably be as curious as we are.' said Penny.

'That maybe true but we must still proceed with caution, Professor James is right, let us see what we can observe first.' said Giles.

They found the path, it looked natural yet they were at odds to explain how it could be so, they started walking up the steep incline which made their calves strain and ache after a little while.

Professor James enjoyed the view across the plain and he saw a few mysterious shapes in the strange purple water. They were still not tired but Professor James started to feel a little hungry and he registered that his legs were now aching.

Onward they marched and finally they were at the top where they discovered a pathway leading into the canyon. They looked across at the building they had seen at a skewed angle down below. It appeared to be an entrance to a city. It had pillars like Georgian buildings, a doorway and windows that looked more like viewing platforms.

'This is all too simple for such a complex structure. I do not like it.'

'What do you mean Uncle James?'

'I mean Penny whatever built these grand abodes were obviously of extreme intelligence, applying logic it makes no sense that we have not encountered one, there is no sentry or look out, I feel a bit like we're-'

'Walking into a trap.' said Gilbert.

'Maybe not quite that dramatic but certainly something.'

'I think you are right Professor.' added Giles.

'So let us tread with stealth.' said Ian.

'There is no need they know we are here, I am sure of it, let us observe and then go in openly perhaps even announce ourselves.'

'It has worked for me plenty of times with strange islands and I have often been welcomed.'

'Is that correct Giles?'

'Ok Professor James, I have also nearly been speared to death a few times as well but who is counting, asides from you?'

Professor James smiled and continued along the ledge. Halfway across they sat down and ate, purposefully watching the Martian building for signs of life. They discussed the power sources and water supply but could see no signs of either, the river flowed naturally past. Some of the docile blue horse like creatures wandered in from the field and one or two disappeared into the buildings but quickly returned outside as if unsure of their territory.

Professor James was wide awake and alert continually assessing the situation, Giles was also and the two men scoured the landscape looking for any minute clue that might indicate what lay ahead.

'Maybe it is abandoned.' said Ian.

'This mystery is most singular, those vegetables must have been planted recently, I think we should be armed from here on out.' said Professor James.

'I agree,' said Professor Giles who already had his gun in his hand. 'The logic makes sense.'

'But let us not shoot the bloody things dead just because they look different from us. Remember we are the guests and technically it is we that are trespassing.'

'Quite right.' said Penny putting her hand on Ian's shoulder.

'We are not here to hunt them but we will take precautions, do not run up to shake their hand, for all we know they could be hostile.' said Giles.

'Let us not get worked up into a frenzy and prepare for battle unnecessarily.'

Professors James and Giles looked at each other

'It is important to be prepared. Remember the story of the island I discovered in Polynesia?' said Giles.

'I think we have had enough death for one trip.'

Penny's comment sobered the mood as they all recalled Dennis.

The party looked for a way across the river as Professor James figured there must be one.

'Look carefully.' cried Ian. 'There is another path against the back wall that leads across and down the ravine, it looks like a giant crack running along the wall.'

As if by magical illusion the pathway appeared and for a minute Professor James wondered whether this was some kind of telepathic planet where things just appeared when needed.

'This all exceedingly clever don't you think?' said Gilbert.

'Yes I do, the only way in is cleverly disguised and beyond that we have no access unless we walk right past their dwellings, if they are hostile we could be in trouble.' said Professor James.

The party traversed along the ledge in silent trepidation mixed with excitement. The walk downhill had their calves hurting as they kept them from running and falling down. As they approached the bottom Professor James felt his hammer cock back and he did not even realise that he had done it. He heard several clicks behind him as others followed suit and at last the team of scientists ventured onto the plain towards the mighty buildings. They saw one of the blue horses dart out toward the meadow and river whilst another strolled inside.

'It is a shame we cannot disguise ourselves as one of them darn horses.' said Ian.

Penny laughed a little too loud but quickly stifled her mouth.

'There is no need to panic, whatever may befall us the one thing I can assure you of is that they know we are here.' said Giles.

Professor James and Giles led the way with their guns drawn toward the empty buildings.

'I think we should announce our arrival. It is polite.' said Giles.

'You are the master of such matters.' replied Professor James.

'*Ahoy there fellow beings, we approach in peace and without hostile intent.*'

The shout echoed around the canyon but the response was an eerie silence.

'*Do you speak English?*'

'I have to say that seems like an alarmingly stupid question.'

'Ok well you bloody try.' said Giles staring at Professor James.

'It was worth a try but there is no need if they wanted to greet us they would.'

Professor James and Giles marched up the steps leading to the doorway of the building. The others followed close behind him and were surprised to see a huge room with a variety of corridors and staircases. Professor James felt rather unsettled at how Earth like it was. He thought about the invention of steps, could anything with their brain capacity conceive of such things, would not ramps always be the rudimentary way to go?

He checked on Penny who was standing there with her mouth wide open and was reminded of the time he had taken her to the zoo as a child, where she kept on holding her mouth open trying to make it as big as a tiger's.

'Fascinating, I never dreamed such a thing could exist on Mars.'

'I was just thinking the same Ian it is so Earth like it has me on edge.' said Giles.

'There is no furniture.' said Gilbert.

'That was my observation.' said Penny.'

'We have a multitude of corridors to choose from. Shall we split up?' said Ian.

'No.' said Giles that may not be wise as we do not know what we are up against.

'Quite.' remarked Professor James.

They had a choice of corridors but Ian made their decision for them by walking towards the left-hand corridor. They came into a room that was filled with bizarre luminescent plants that almost appeared to be electrical trunking. There were drawings etched into the wall and a strange language written on some kind of parchment. Platforms, gantries and staircases created a maze. Penny walked over to some of the writing on the wall and began to sketch it.

'This is beyond what I could have dreamed.' cried Ian.

'It has us all dumbstruck I think.' said Giles.

'They are vastly intelligent. Could this place have been abandoned?'

'Doubt it.' said Giles 'Although there must be very organised as there are not many objects scattered about, what is the purpose of the room do you think?'

'This room seems to have no purpose.' said Gilbert.

'Every room has a purpose.' Penny said shouting across it.

'It is not beyond the realms of possibility that this room is superfluous but what is all the writing, what are the weird looking plants everywhere and how come they are bio luminescent?' said Professor James.

'Perhaps this place is abandoned and they are some kind of invasive alien weed that has taken over.' said Giles.

'That would hold credit except look at the way it has grown; it looks organised. Why has it not covered the front of the property like creepers?'

'I agree.' said Giles 'Something is off kilter, your initial instincts were right Professor James, I can feel it now.'

They climbed a staircase that was made of an alien substance the like of which they had not seen before. It was hard and tough yet seemed somehow flexible. After following a gantry they came to an off shoot that led through to another area.

They walked along the corridor and came out onto another platform, they saw what looked akin to a huge tree trunk, the width of a house, it was pulsing and writhing as if a million bioluminescent worms had been poured into a glass tube.

'Look.' cried Penny 'buildings, more buildings.'

Professor James looked over the railing and could see rows of houses that looked as grand as the front, they were bathed in a beautiful sunset red and near the bottom some of them were white as if made out of chalk.

'It is like a honeycomb, this is not a species of creature, it is a civilisation.' said Giles.

'And look, that tree in the middle must be their power source the routes are leading off to each level.' said Ian.

'It is so odd that we have not seen anyone?' said Gilbert.

'I would like to do some reconnaissance to see if I can determine who and what they are and perhaps a bit about their nature.' said Giles.

'I just thought, perhaps they are invisible?'

'Don't be absurd Penny.' said Professor James.

'We cannot say for certain that they are not.' said Ian.

'It would account for us not seeing anybody.' said Gilbert.

'Yes Gilbert and that would explain your uneasy feeling Professor James'

'My dear Penny I really do not think-'

'What is it Professor.' said Gilbert walking forward and holding the railing that looked like metal but felt like wood.

'I was going to say, have a thousand eyes on us, I do not think they are invisible but what if they are able to watch us without been seen?'

'Why haven't they stopped us?' said Ian.

'We could be the ones who are being studied.' said Giles.

'That is a creepy thought.' said Penny stretching her arms.

'Do you suppose that humans have already somehow reached here and colonised it?' said Gilbert.

'The same thought crossed my mind but much of this is too unrecognisable with the exception of the staircases and platforms and building fronts.'

They reached the staircase and descended, when they got down to the first dwelling level they were alarmed at how big it was.

They walked down the cavern and past the front entrances, weird lights shone from within, they kept on walking and at the end of the row of houses was a tunnel. The team briefly discussed their options and all agreed that the main shaft was the priority.

As they walked back toward the central staircase, Penny selected a house for them to go into, they knocked first as it seemed like the right thing to do as they were curious investigators and not trespassers in Professor James' mind. Inside was a strange room that had seats and lights both formed by plants along with a strange rectangle on the wall that looked like a blank canvas.

There were some obvious similarities to humanity except no pictures, etchings or decorations upon the wall. In another room they saw bowls of strange fruits and what they assumed to be food, there were no cupboards but weird shelves created with plant membrane, through the rooms they ventured but found no beds.

'It seems very basic.' said Penny.

'It is rather fascinating if you ask me.'

'I am with you Ian.' said Gilbert.

'I cannot fathom it unless this is not a dwelling.' said Giles.

'We see only what we want to see and we judge only by what we know. This is an advanced civilisation I am sure of it but we do not know what we are looking for or at.' said Professor James.

'Let us try another house.' said Gilbert.

'Let us try another floor.' said Giles.

'Yes, that would make more sense.' said Penny.

'We should press on to see if it really is a city at the bottom and then plan what we shall do. Whether we should try and get a night's sleep here or whether we should journey all the way back and sleep in the ship which would be a very safe option.' said Giles.

The party headed down to the next floor and found more dwellings, as they went down another couple of levels they started to notice a change.

'The inhabitant's spaces are getting nicer the further we go down.' said Penny.

'Well observed. I do believe you are right.' said Professor James.

'The rooms are lot more spacious and the level of detail seems to be more refined. What is that bizarre contraption in the middle of the room?' said Ian.

'It looks like some kind of fountain or liquid delivery device.' said Gilbert.

'Yes, it is intriguing isn't it, let us see what it does.'

'Steady on Penny not yet, we still have much to see and document and until I see what we are dealing with let us not take anything for granted.' said Giles.

'It is not the time to let our guard down.' said Professor James.

'Something just moved I swear it.' said Ian swigging from his hip flask and wiping his mouth on his sleeve.

'Are you sure?' said Giles with furrowed eyebrows.

'I am not drunk if that is what you are thinking.'

'By Jove, he is right, something just moved in my periphery as well.' said Gilbert.

'What do you think it could be?'

'It could be anything Penny.' said Giles.

'Quite.' said Professor James walking forward, his muscles tensed, he had been feeling uneasy all morning, he was attuned to danger and things being out of place and knew there was something dreadfully wrong. Whether it was malevolent or not he could not tell. He walked around a strange artefact placed in the middle of the room that appeared to be a workbench and looked about, he could see nothing.

'Where?' inquired Professor James walking back around the other side.

'It just caught my eye.' said Gilbert shrugging his shoulders.

'I think it was on the floor.' said Ian.

'Let us all stand in a line and look together, if anything moves, we will spot it.'

As they watched an insect the size of a large frog came out from around the table object, it was khaki brown and looked akin to a beetle with large antlers, it had ten spindly legs that appeared to be spikes.

'An insect how fascinating.' said Ian.

'Stop.' said Professor James as Penny went to approach it.

'It is just an insect.'

'Penny, do as you are told.'

Penny's cheeks flushed red but she remained silent.

'Look, it is rearing up like a tarantula.' said Gilbert.

'Acting just like a creature on Earth when it's threatened.' said Giles.

'I do not care I am leading this expedition and no one is to go near until I say so.'

'I think you are over reacting Professor.' said Gilbert.

'It is just an insect, have we got a jar big enough to collect him, he would make a fascinating study.' said Ian.

'I agree.' said Penny.

'That is bloody enough from both you, confound you.'

'They are just making an observation.' said Giles.

'I don't care just-'

Professor James pushed Penny as hard he could, she slammed straight in Gilbert and Ian who stumbled back as Penny fell to the floor. The huge scythe just missed her and they were now facing a seven-foot-tall insect.

XIII Denizens of the Deep

Professor James drew his machete, countered the next blow but it did not slice off the mighty antler as expected and he swung to the other side to deflect a hit from its other one. Professor James knew he could not defend both antlers at once and was aware that he was about to be sliced in two. Giles got there just in time. The two men looked at each other and together kicked the giant insect with all their might straight in the centre of the body, the insect not expecting it, buckled over and fell backwards. It squirmed on its back trying to right itself.

Gilbert walked forward with his gun out but Professor James stopped him.

'Just run.'

They all ran outside and were glad to find there was not a welcome party waiting for them.

The group ran back to the platform as fast as they could and once there stopped to look behind them. The creature was not in pursuit, they descended a couple of levels and then tried their luck again. The dwellings were definitely getting more glamourous and larger, they had just begun to discuss the potential hierarchal structure when another insect appeared, this time there was no hesitation, they made for the door and back to the apparent safety of the main staircase.

They descended another level and saw more insects just off the platform that led to the dwellings.

'They are standing guard.' said Ian.

'Yes, that is exactly what they're doing.' said Professor James. 'Let us keeping moving quickly, if they did not know we're here, they certainly do now.'

They followed the staircase downwards past many levels of gantries and dwellings to the bottom where they found wide pathways, strange looking doorways and a city full of buildings.

'Why is it empty?' said Penny. 'It is making me uneasy.'

'We all feel the same Penny you can be assured of that.' remarked Giles.

'I have just had a thought' said Gilbert.

'Do continue.' said Professor James not taking his eyes off the city in front of them.

'Perhaps we have met this civilisation already.'

'What do you mean?' said Ian.

'The insects.' replied Gilbert.

'It is certainly a possibility.' said Giles

'You mean those giant insect creatures built all this?' said Penny.

'Why not?' replied Gilbert.

'What do you think Professor James?'

'I was about to ask your opinion Giles. Whilst it is a distinct possibility I am not convinced, the doors are large but they do not seem to be the right dimensions.'

'How so?' asked Ian.

'Well, the height may be correct but I do not think the width is. Not with the giant claws that they had.'

'Perhaps they turn as they walk in.'

'No, I do not think so Penny, if you were building a house would you make it inconvenient for yourself to enter?'

'Ah yes Professor James but perhaps they shrink down to insect size when they enter and then become large again inside.'

'Then why have large doorways?' replied he.

'It would be a lot more secure to have tiny holes leading into large dwellings.' said Giles.

'And look how wide the pathways are between these structures?' said Ian.

'Well it is a possibility.' said Penny.

'No one is saying it is erroneous Penny we just think it an unlikely prospect at the moment.' said Gilbert smiling at her.

'Look there is one of those blue horses again.' said Giles pointing into the city.

'Those horses are not afraid of anything, they roam this world free and uninterrupted.' said Ian.

'They must be docile and friendly and let us not forget so would horses on Earth, if we let them.' said Penny.

'Quite.' said Professor James rubbing his chin.

'Do you think it is foolhardy to continue?' said Gilbert.

'Nonsense, we shall not stop that I tell you.' said Ian waving his index finger.

Giles and Professor James walked forward a couple of steps.

'I think we should be careful, but to turn back now would be fruitless after we have come all this way. This tribe, whatever they are, are intelligent enough to have guards and as Professor James correctly surmised earlier, they have been watching us for a while, it would be logical to assume they could certainly capture or kill us as we tried to retreat.'

Professor James took out a biscuit and bit into it, the crunch seemed enormously loud within the giant crater.

'Not the only reason for continuing. If they were as savage as we suppose then why have they not killed us already?' said Professor James.

'Perhaps they are afraid of us.'

'Perhaps Penny.' said Giles.

'I don't care whether they are or not, I want to meet one and confabulate with it.' said Ian.

'Then let us push on.' said Gilbert.

'Hurrah.' cried Giles stifling himself as the word echoed.

The staircase opened up to a strange road that was made of rock but had some kind of brown algae on it that made it pleasant and spongy to walk on. They walked to the end of the road and into the city. There seemed to be no concept of transport, no bicycles or trains, no strange creatures tied up. Professor James wondered whether that was why they kept seeing the blue horses wandering around but he could not spot any kind of harness. Professor James also noted the absence of the insects they had seen on the gantries above.

They looked into some buildings and saw loads of the plant membrane that they had earlier, there was also strange tubes running around. Down the road they saw another dwelling that almost resembled offices. There were buildings that had rooms that looked akin to bars and restaurants yet they could not see any food and the furniture was misshapen and did not appear to hold any particular form.

They progressed to the centre of the city where there was a huge temple in the middle. It had pillars that would not have been out of place in ancient Greece and large malformed steps. There was some kind of writing similar to what they had seen earlier. As they walked around several of the blue horses stopped in the doorway. They did not do anything just stood there.

Professor James held up his hand and they all stopped.

'I have been a confounded lunatic, idiot, fool.' said he through gritted teeth and flushed cheeks.

'Steady on old chap.' said Giles 'What's the matter?'

Professor James ignored the question and looked behind him, more horses lazily strolled toward them.

'I thought those houses were empty.' cried Penny.

'So did I.' said Ian.

Giles scratched his knee and looked up with a bewildered look on his face.

'The hips, look at the hips man.' said Professor James.

Giles' face collapsed and his mouth dropped open.

'What is happening?' said Penny stepping close to her uncle.

The horses stopped and the team realised that they had become surrounded.

'That is what had been bothering me Giles, I knew there was something amiss about their structure, even the way they walked.'

'What are you talking about?' asked Ian.

'I think I realise what is happening but what have their legs got to do with it?' said Gilbert.

'They are not strictly quadrupedal.' said Giles

'No, they are also bipedal.' said Professor James.

As he said it the two horses in the doorway stood up on two legs and moved aside to let a third one come out on to the top of the stairs. They could feel a commotion behind them and upon turning around saw that they had all stood up as well.

'Good God, you mean to say these horses are the race that we have been looking for the whole time?' said Ian.

'Quite.' remarked Professor James with his eyes locked on the front creature in the doorway.

It was almost human in its stance and its powerful front limbs had transformed into formidable arms that were muscular and tense. Professor James guessed that they were immensely strong. Its dual trunk hid a mouth underneath it, its eyes were large and upon closer inspection the darkest shade of brown, not quite the black he first observed. He realised the sausage like toes now served as the perfect fingers. The creature walked down two steps.

'How shall we handle this Giles?'

'I think we should be amenable and friendly. There is no evidence of hostility yet.'

'I agree. Nobody draw your weapon.' said Professor James snapping his head toward Gilbert who was just about to draw it.

The creature stood there looking at them, the other blue horses stood perfectly still and horizontal, it reminded Professor James of the Queen's guards. Professor James walked forward two steps to match the creature's own behaviour. The thing tilted its head as if trying to understand the intentions of the invader.

'Bow.' said Giles.

Professor James heeded the advice and bowed slightly, he felt it was the right thing to do if they were going to get out of this place alive, he had been assessing the situation and considered how far into Mars they had wandered and that they had been watched the whole way, the Martians clearly had communicative and organisational abilities. The risk was great even without the other wildlife they had also encountered. Dennis flashed through his thoughts and instantly Professor James was replaying his death, the professor gritted his teeth and forced it out of his mind.

To his surprise the creature reciprocated the gesture, it walked down another two steps, Professor James mimicked and Giles stepped forward two paces to keep up with Professor James. The creature at the front stepped forward again and to the party's astonishment held out its hand.

Professor James turned around to Giles who shrugged his shoulders, Ian, Gilbert and Penny looked at each other in stunned silence.

Professor James walked straight toward the creature and extended his hand, he then used his left hand to place on the creature's arm to indicate that he was keen, warm and friendly. The skin of the arm felt taut and had a peculiar rubber quality to it. The hands were large and firm and from his initial glance he could see that the rolls of flesh that served as fingers had something more to them and Professor James wondered whether they were telescopic.

The other two creatures came down from the doorway and so did the rest of the party. Ian shook its hand and had tears in his eyes, one of them betrayed him and made a run for it down his weathered face. Professor James gently placed his hand on his shoulder as he knew what this meant to him.

'You have been vindicated my friend.'

Ian ignored Professor James comments, walked forward and shook the lead creatures' hand again with a solid gesture as if they were firm associates with a long history.

'Hallo, we are man, the race of Earth, do you understand us in anyway?'

The creature shook its head.

'How did it know to shake its head?'

'I don't know Gilbert but there are too many coincidences for my liking.' said Professor James.

'We are scientists we do not believe in coincidence.' said Giles.

'Quite.' said Professor James turning his attention back to the creature. 'We are a peaceful tribe and never seek to harm.'

'Are you sure about that?' said Gilbert.

Giles shot a hard stare in Gilbert's direction.

'There is much we can learn about your world and the many species that live upon it, will you accommodate our presence as investigative scientists?'

'You are wasting your time Giles.' said Professor James.

The other creatures had all begun to come nearer.

'Perhaps we could draw as they obviously possess a fantastic degree of intelligence.' said Penny.

The creatures grew close to Penny and leaned in. Professor James shot his arm out and pushed her back.

'I think you are a hit young lady.' said Ian.

'I hope this is not a male dominated planet.'

'I doubt that Giles, I am the only girl here, they are probably curious as to why I look so different.'

'We had better keep a close eye on her.' said Professor James to Giles who turned his head and nodded in reply.

'I do not need special attention; now stop embarrassing me.'

The creature motioned for them to follow and walked up the steps and into the large temple. Inside was a nerve centre of giant machines that contained mechanics not like anything on Earth and the plant membranes they had seen in the dwellings earlier had weird writing on them as if there was some way of displaying things upon them. It was the same strange alien language they had encountered earlier. The creatures were hard at work pushing buttons, pulling leavers and squeezing plant heads that seemed to act as some kind of activating device.

'This technology is way beyond anything we could ever comprehend.' said Ian.

'The mathematical equations would take centuries to discover and decipher.' said Gilbert walking forward to a screen that had a code on it consisting of lines, dashes and dots.

'It is so exciting don't you think uncle?' said Penny.

Professor James turned his head and looked at his niece who had a huge smile on her face.

'Don't tell me – Quite.' she added.

Giles laughed out loud and their hosts all turned around startled. Giles held his hands out in gesture and after a couple of seconds hesitation they all resumed what they were doing.

The lead creature beckoned them forward.

'It sets me on edge how they know human mannerisms.' said Professor James.

'Perhaps theirs is the same as ours. There is nothing illogical about our body language.' said Gilbert.

'I wonder why they do not have any identifying garments.'

'What do you mean Ian?' said Penny.

'Do you mean like dress or something to signify rank?'

'Yes Gilbert that is correct?'

'That is an astute point Ian, I was just wondering the same thing, assuming the one we are following has some kind of important rank.'

'There seems to be no animosity at least.' said Giles.

'We need to study them. How are we supposed to communicate?' said Ian.

'Maybe that is where he is taking us.' said Professor James.

'I doubt it.' said Gilbert.

They walked through various banks filled with workers and into a long corridor, at the end they came out onto a platform where the creature motioned for them to stop. The group did as instructed and the platform lowered itself down, they could see many more different levels, Professor James began to realise just how vast this empire was.

As they walked along a giant platform, Giles nudged Professor James in the ribs and nodded to their left, Professor James quickly looked and through a cavernous hole in the rock he could see a field of a strange alien crop being harvested.

'They are as industrial as man.' whispered Giles.

'I wonder whether they are as ambitious.'

'We shall see.'

They continued on looking through every cavern and doorway and saw more fields and purple meteorite. This was of great intrigue as it looked to be the same as the green comet that they used to get to Mars, the only difference was the colour. Professor James immediately wondered whether it possessed the same qualities. The green super oxygen giving plants grew in abundance everywhere and Professor James guessed that it was these plants that were the sole source of life as well as the water.

Eventually the creature stopped and bade them through a small archway, when they came out of the other side they found themselves next to a lagoon where a huge cascading waterfall loomed high above them and strange glowing plants and trees surrounded the pool of water, there was a beach and what they took to be tables and chairs. Strange flying creatures danced in and out of the spray which created a rainbow of reds, greens and purples.

XIV A Beautiful Imposition

Professor James pulled out a cigarette, Giles took one and lit up as well. The creature that had guided them studied closely what they were doing. Ian took a swig from his hip flask.

'Ian, if you are going back on the hard stuff you can bloody well share it.' said Professor James.

'Fair enough.' said Ian handing it over like a disappointed child being forced to share his sweets.

The creature leant forward and its two small stubby trunks breathed some of the smoke in, it retreated and bolted for the water, drank some and then snorted it out in jets. This brought much needed laughter to the group.

The creature motioned for them to sit down, the chairs felt soft and squidgy but comfortable. A second and third creature had come out and sat with them. They waved clumsily as they sat down.

'You cannot understand us?' asked Penny.

The creature shrugged his shoulders.

'But how do you know to shrug your shoulders; have you been to Earth?' said Ian.

The creature looked at them and shrugged its shoulders.

'Well we know that they drink the water at least.'

'I do not think we should be too near water after our encounter earlier.' said Giles.

'Poor Dennis would have loved to see this.' said Gilbert looking out at the waterfall.

'That reminds me when we get a moment of privacy, we must check our supplies, we are a long way from the craft and must ensure that we have enough for the return journey.' said Giles.

'Look, one of them is bringing something over.' said Penny.

One of the creatures brought over a tray with cups made from leaves so fine that they were transparent, there was also some strange looking fruit that looked like a plum but twice the size and brown in colour. The host offered them some. Giles looked at Professor James.

'We must heed caution Giles we do not know what it contains, it may be harmless to them but lethal to us and the same goes for offering them ours.'

Professor James did his best to mime that it might hurt them. Penny and Giles found it distinctly funny and they could see Professor James' cheeks turning florid at their laughter.

The creature looked unperturbed but frustration grew within the party at the lack of communication. Professor James sensed that their hosts felt the same, it almost seemed pointless, why bother coming to Mars if you cannot communicate with its fore leading denizens.

'You know this is what I would picture heaven to look like maybe with a yellow sun in the sky.' said Ian looking around.

'It seems a little Earth like to me.' said Penny 'You have the dominant species and the animals that are all subservient or certainly not of equal intelligence. We know that they are intelligent but to what degree do they judge morality?'

'Pray continue.' said Gilbert.

'Well we know that they are technical and industrial but there seems to be no distinction between them, have you actually seen anyone give an order?'

'This is brilliant observation Penny.' said Giles.

'It is also as if they all move in synch. They know what to do and how to act forthwith without any protest or compunction?'

'Why compunction?' asked Gilbert.

'Surmising that if they act upon what they deem to be necessity or perhaps a single desire they would act without compunction without the forethought of whether it was morally correct.'

'You have taken a lot of liberties in that statement Penny don't you think?' said Ian.

'Perhaps, but my mother took me to see a swimming team once at the baths and they moved with such precision and grace one had to wonder how they achieved it.'

'With practice they learn the routine.'

'Of course Ian but that does not mean that mind synchronisation is not possible in an alien species.'

'Telepathy?'

'Yes Uncle James, what if they do not need to speak?'

'It is a possibility as there are some possible cases of it on Earth.' remarked he.

'Or further to that what if they are linked to one single mind so how we might move one hand in one direction yet a leg in another so this mind rather than controlling limbs controls a race of creatures.'

'Interesting theory but I am not sure that is correct as there is obviously some form of hierarchy and your theory does not lend to that.' said Professor James.

'How do you know?' said Penny crossing her arms.

'The dwellings, remember the lower we got the nicer they became, there is obviously some kind of class system here.' said Professor James.

Ian clapped his hands. 'Well I think you're the most erudite student I have yet to encounter.'

'Here, here.' said Gilbert.

Professor James and Giles were locked in a side conversation, they discussed the telepathy theory and it struck both of them that they had not heard any noises from the creatures yet – were they deaf? It seemed highly unlikely albeit they could not see any ears, but they were very alert as they had seen out on the plains. Giles was intent in finding out about all the plants and animals so he could catalogue them and add it to his ever-growing encyclopaedia of natural wonders. James was more preoccupied with their technology, what could they do and what was there for man to discover? Was cancer on this planet and had they cured it? What properties did the purple meteorites have? Were they more advanced than the green ones? Professor James' mind whirred like the sail of a windmill during a gale. He had to befriend them but how do you do that when there is no language to be shared between you.

There was still too much they did not know, why did they let them get so far in without introducing themselves? It seemed a trite too convenient for them to be allowed to wander right into their sanctuary. Professor James was convinced that they had studied their every move since they entered the kingdom; so why would they allow them to enter right into the heart of their domain.

A thought crossed his mind like a black cat shooting across his path. Perhaps they were the ones being studied and what if they were being led to their demise? The problem gnawed at him as he could not be certain of hostility and as an experienced adventurer and scientist he knew he was onto the most significant scientific find since the invention of the wheel, he was loathe to ruin it through human paranoia and circumstantial evidence.

Professor James looked up and as he did one of the creatures lifted his drink, held it towards him and then drank some.

'He just gave me a toast, this cannot be coincidence, confound it, they know of human behaviours I am sure of it.' said Professor James.

'The evidence is damning if you ask me.' said Ian rubbing his eyes.

'Penny, draw them something.'

'Ooh that's a good idea Giles what shall I draw?'

'Draw the planets marking us and them and then indicate that we have travelled to their planet.'

Penny drew the planets and tried her best to get the outlay of countries on Earth and the volcanoes on Mars. She showed it to the one that had led them there, it leant forward and examined it, the Martian looked up at Penny and Penny took her pencil and pointed at Earth, she pointed at herself and moved the pencil across to Mars, she looked at the creature who she only knew in her head as the blue horse, without warning it nodded its head.

He motioned to Mars and pointed to himself.

Professor James had to stifle a response of 'yes we bloody know that.'

The Martian pointed at the Earth and waved his hands.

'What does that mean?' said Giles.

Penny leant forward and looked the creature in the eyes. It looked at them again and waved its hands.

'Is he telling us goodbye?' said Ian.

'Or to go home.' said Gilbert brushing something off his trousers.

The Martian leant forward and pointed to Penny's pencil. She gave it to him and he took it and crossed out the Earth.

They all looked at each other.

'What is that supposed to mean?' said Giles.

'Let us not leap to conclusions.' said Gilbert

'It is a bit ominous.' said Professor James.

'It does not seem to be sinister, its body language has not changed and hordes of guards or insects have not appeared.' said Ian.

The Martian leaned forward and tried to speak but it just made a lot of guttural noises.

'It must have a completely different voice box to us.' said Penny.

'It is incapable of speech.' said Ian with a deep frown upon his face.

Gilbert pulled out some bread and a little pot of jam.

'We might as well take of advantage of the rest.' said he.

Professor James nodded and they all got their food out and began to eat, they offered the Martians some food but they did not accept. Professor James motioned to them they did not know whether they could eat and it appeared they understood.

'I was thinking Giles, perhaps we could take some of their food back with us and run some tests then we may be able to determine whether it is safe enough to eat upon our return.'

'Yes, I have been thinking about that and I think there is a probability that some of it would be safe, it is organic and for fruit to grow there must be certain elements involved, all of which are palatable to us.'

'One of the biggest factors for the growing of fruit is absent.' said Penny.

'She is right you know Giles.' said Professor James putting some jam on a cracker and noisily biting into it.

'What is this factor?' asked Ian.

'I was about to ask that.' said Gilbert.

'The sun, the whole world is subterranean, how do they grow?' replied Penny.

'Clever observation Penny but what about carrots and potatoes?'

'They still require sunlight for the leaves above.' said Professor James realising that he was warm and subterranean caverns on Earth were usually cool.

'So how do we find out whether that was a threat against our planet back then?' said Giles looking at their hosts.

'I have been thinking about that.' said Ian.

'Yes, so have I.' said Professor James.

'I do not think they intend to harm us, they are wonderful creatures if you ask me, simply wonderous as is this whole world.'

'Ian will you cut back on the drink damnit.'

'I am sober enough thank you James.' said Ian looking Professor James in the eye.

Professor James felt his anger rising.

'Well I have been thinking what if it means something more cryptic like they cannot go to Earth or perhaps they simply do not know what we are referring to?' said Gilbert.

'That is an excellent point, maybe they do not know they are in a solar system or that there are other planets.' said Professor James.

'There must be some way to communicate with them surely.' said Giles.

'We need to study that writing on the wall.' said Professor James.

'Looked more like symbols if you ask me.' said Gilbert.

'Perhaps that is how they write.' said Penny 'I have already been giving it some thought and besides we have made a breakthrough, even if it is very small.'

'My hunch says he knows more about us than we do about them.' said Giles lighting a cigarette and returning the favour to Professor James by offering him one.

'So does mine.' said Professor James accepting the gift.

'I will draw the craft and show us leaving Earth so they know how we got there.' said Penny.

'What a fantastic idea, we could take one or two of them back with us, imagine lecturing back at Oxford with two extra-terrestrials in tow?' said Ian.

Professor James saw his old friend running down the corridor in his lab coat and remembered what a fine-looking chap he once was, Professor James looked up and was grieved to see the old withered and broken man he had become. He felt that sometimes vindication comes too late, no matter how much he was applauded and celebrated on their return, he would never be the man he was and in the deep chasms of his soul he knew that Ian knew it as well.

'Ian my old friend. It would not be wise for us to do that?'

'Why not, By Jove, we may learn something about them.' said Ian throwing beer out of his bottle as he swung his arms.

'Granted. But if they do not know we have a craft is it wise for us to point it out to them?'

'I feel quite inferior for not being first to point that out.' said Giles 'There has been many a time when I was glad we hid the boat.'

'Makes sense, after all, we have no other way home do we?' said Gilbert.

'It all seems so final now, I am really enjoying this and now I am wondering if we will ever get home.' said Penny.

'Poppycock, that's what I think, confounded poppycock. We should take them to our ship, with their technology they may be able to improve it, how do we even know it will get us home? We have come to this wonderful planet, found an astounding race of civilised creatures and all you can wonder is are they hostile?'

'I appreciate your sentiment Ian but there have been many a time when I have been proved wrong and without justification as well. One of the most horrifying things that I saw was a missionary climb off a boat and walk up a beach with a big smile on face, his arms were open wide and he had a bible in his hand, they returned his kind greeting by throwing a spear into his chest, killing him instantly.'

'Oh that is horrible.' said Penny dropping her pad and covering her face.

'It haunts me to this day. The point I make is from my vast experience there is a never a reason not to add a thread of caution to proceedings.'

'I think you're all cowards.'

'Ian, what the hell has got into you?' said Professor James.

'Nothing.' said he looking away.

They all looked at each other.

'So it is agreed,' said Gilbert 'that we extend every courtesy but heed caution.'

'It does sound wise.' said Penny picking her pad and pencil back up again.

'We should also be careful what we discuss in front of them?' said Giles.

'In case they understand us?' said Professor James instinctively adopting a defensive stance.

'I had not thought of that, we have no way of telling but what I meant is they are intelligent enough to detect mood changes, postures and body language like we can read animals behaviour, there is not one of us who does not know what their horse is thinking.'

'Very apt description.'

'They are not horses confound you, confound you all, I will strike you down I swear it.' said Ian getting up and threatening Gilbert with a bottle, Gilbert recoiled but Professor James was straight out of his chair.'

'*What the blasted hell do you think you are doing man? If you were not my friend I would punch the living daylights out of you, so help me God.*'

Ian looked at his friend and burst in to tears. He sobbed uncontrollably like a three year old who had just been told off. There was not much that caught Professor James by surprise these days but this did. He stood there dumbfounded for a few seconds and then dropped his temper and his guard.

'Come here you old fool. What has gotten into you man? Are you having some kind of breakdown or something? You are on Mars Ian, do you understand me, Mars. Keep your wits about you. I told you not to drink it didn't I?'

'*I am not drunk damn it.*' said he.

'Ian I know a drunk man when I see one.' said Giles who marched over in case Professor James needed support.

'I'm alright, really.' said Ian pulling on the lapels of his lab coat.

'Well this is being confiscated I don't care what you damned say.' said Professor James snatching out the whisky flask from Ian's lab coat pocket. Two things immediately surprised Professor James as he retrieved the item, the first was that Ian put up no fight and the second was that the hip flask was heavy.

'It's almost full.' said Professor James throwing it to Giles.

'He refilled it earlier.' said Penny.

'Yes but we helped him finish that. I have been keeping watch he shouldn't be this drunk.' said Professor James.

'He must be inebriated he reeks of drink.' said Giles.

'He always reeks of drink.' said Gilbert standing up and snatching the flask out of Giles's hand.

'Why did you almost attack me for and with a bottle you fiend.'

'I'm sorry Gilbert, I really am, I do not know what came over me.'

'If he attacks one of the Martians we could all be in for it.' said Penny.

Professor James turned to look at their hosts and for the first time saw them in fierce discussion. They spoke clicks, beats and guttural noises and Professor James found it unsettling that he had only just seen them converse. It made him wonder what else he did not know. His hosts had sat there still and patient whilst they sat and discussed everything right in front of them, perhaps they could understand English after all?

The lead creature stood up, waved his hand and pleaded for them all to go with him. Professor James grabbed Ian's arm and led them forcefully away.

'He must have had an extra fill up somewhere.' said Penny.

The creature led them through to another area through tunnels and corridors, they saw more caverns with great fields, life giving plants and much more of the purple crystal meteorite which they were all desperate to get a sample of.

Eventually they came into a giant room that once again looked like a control centre there was a huge plant membrane suspended in the air, it warped and wobbled and then an image appeared.

'Good God that is Earth.' said Gilbert.

XV The Lethal Inquiry

'It is not just Earth, that looks like Kensington, it is look, there is Gloucester Road and Cromwell Road,' said Professor James.

'And there is Queens Gate.' said Penny.

'They have technology then.' said Giles.

'The screen wobbled and the images changed it showed a man waving and a lady beckoning.'

'That is how they knew our body language.' said Penny.

'They have been spying on us, spying on us, oh how I want to dance and sing for joy.'

'Pull yourself together Ian.' said Professor James.

'I wonder what else we do not know. We cannot see onto other planets like that.' said Giles.

'I wonder why they are showing us.' said Penny.

'Well done Penny. Why? Is often the most important question to ask.' said Professor James.

'Unless you're lost at sea and then it is where?' said Giles.

Penny sniggered.

Professor James rolled his eyes and watched Ian marvelling at everything, his eyes seemed empty and distant as if his soul had already departed from him. Professor

James changed his feelings from anger to immense concern, had it all got too much for the old man after a lifetime of humiliation and alcohol, was his mockery not complete?

The Martians played moving pictures of life on Earth, they zoomed out and saw Earth just like they had when they first left its atmosphere. Professor James tried to take it all in and relax a bit, it was difficult as he was worried about his niece and his old friend who seemed to be disintegrating before his very eyes.

Professor James watched to his utter amazement as he saw their craft heading away from it. He couldn't help but worry how flimsy it looked.

'Confound it they have the power to record imagery and from anywhere in space but how By Jove?' cried Gilbert.

Ian burst out laughing.

'That is what I would like to know?' said Professor James.

'This is way beyond what we expected.' said Penny.

'Indeed it is Penny.' said Gilbert drinking some more of Ian's whisky and surprised that he did not notice or try to take it.

'But are we flies to the trap of Venus? That is what I want to know.' said Giles.

Professor James looked at his friend but it did not utter a word for they both felt like they were being studied under a microscope.

'Why are you showing us this?' said Professor James.

The lead Martian let out a series of bleats and Professor James read frustration in its eyes. Professor James shrugged his shoulders in the hope of a reaction. It showed a picture of Mars and then went back to Earth, the creature held up its finger for Mars and down for Earth.

'How do we not read this as open hostility?' said Giles.

'I don't know, they are not attacking us but my gun is cocked and my cutlass unstrapped.'

'The thing that bothers me is what they are trying to say, I suspect they have been trying to tell us something ever since we arrived and I just cannot make up my mind whether they are friend or foe. It is hard to rationalise as everything is so different to what we know and it is easy to jump to conclusions. Giles, I think we will have to head home anyway I fear that Ian is losing his mind or something.'

'I share your concerns but he is just really drunk, the excitement got the better of him, always tries to hide himself from swigging the beer.' said Giles.

'I suspect that was modesty and necessity.'

'Look.' shrieked Penny. 'Is that Mount Olympus?'

'Yes Penny. The largest volcano known to man.' said Ian.

They all stood and stared at the close up of the volcano, its icy tor standing like a sculpture for the stars with its rocky red slopes, a million tracks and contours, trails for the Gods.

'It is so amazing I just have to sketch it.' Penny said holding up her hand to the Martian.

The Martian's eyes widened and increased, it seemed to Professor James that it smiled and took favour on her for it turned to another Martian, said something and the image stayed put.

Penny sat there drawing earnestly, Penny was a great inspirational painter, putting her own light and touch into the world that she sees. Professor James seeing the Martians were distracted studied the environment they were in.

Penny finished her drawing and the Martians clapped their hands, now he had seen their moving images Professor James wondered just how much they understood. Their actions were appropriately timed so he had to assume that they understood the basic body language of humans.

She offered it to the Martians as a gift, they bowed and took it from her, then he bade them to follow once again, they carried on walking and found Ian was starting to wander off on his own course and they had to pull him back in.

They came to a great chasm that fell down for many fathoms and the bottom was full of the purple meteorite that created jagged rocks, they had to walk around the lip and could not help but think the same question, with all the railings the Martians had everywhere, why wasn't there any railings here?

'If you think I am going to get some purple samples from down there, you're mistaken, mightily mistaken Ian.' said Giles.

'I'll go.' said Ian walking over to the edge.

Professor James yanked him back. 'No you will not you are to stay with me. I do wish you would sober up old man you are testing the limit of my endurance and our friendship might I add.'

Ian looked at him and gave a laugh.

Professor James ignored him and carried on walking, having had a quick look down the chasm for himself and growing ever more convinced that they would never find their way out on their own if they needed to.

They entered another room and Professor James was surprised to see a lot more Martians in there, he grew a little apprehensive when they closed in behind them, it was as if they were gathering to watch something.

Another screen came up and showed Earth, this time the Martian ran its finger across its throat, Giles and Professor James looked at each other, what did this mean?

A picture of Mars appeared and he held his thumb up.

'They are going to destroy Earth? They want us to live on Mars or they do not want us to leave? What the hell is that supposed to mean, they have all this bloody technology and we cannot tell what the hell they are babbling on about.' cried Gilbert.

'They are only there to be worshipped as the creators of chaos and wonder.'

'In your case I think you will find that is whisky Ian.' said Giles.

This brought a snigger from Penny and Gilbert.

'Laugh my friends, laugh all you want like pixies in the St James park but you will never see as I see now, the wonderful truth of what I see now.'

'We need to head home and fast there is something not right with him and I do not believe it to be drunkenness, it is more that than firewater that has got hold of him.'

'Are you sure old man?'

'Giles, I have known that man my whole life and seen him drunk on many occasion that is not his personality drunk or sober, something is wrong I know it is and to ignore it would be foolhardy we should have turned back when Dennis died and now someone else is not faring well. I shall not continue.'

'Let them finish showing us what they have to show then we can politely explain that we have to go.' said Giles.

The Martian was pointing to a picture of Mars and Earth and putting his hand on his chest, the upper torso was magnificently cut with muscle and as much as they relaxed Professor James never forgot how strong they probably are.

Professor James noticed movement amongst the Martians. He looked at Giles for support, Giles acknowledged the glance with a shrug of his shoulders. The Martian bought up another screen of Earth and waved towards them all.

They watched as once again the Martian motioned to his mouth and waved his arms away as if blowing a kiss.

'What bizarre behaviour.' said Gilbert.

'Perhaps he is blowing us a kiss, don't forget, they have seen our behaviour on Earth.'

'But he is not pointing at anyone?' said Professor James.

'Maybe he means it to all of us Giles.'

'Penny, do you really think that creature is blowing us a kiss?' said Giles.

'It seemed more to be a kiss outward into the air like you see opera singers do at the end of a performance.' said Gilbert.

'You mean it is expecting a standing ovation?' replied Giles.

'All I am saying is that is what it looks like to me.' said Gilbert scratching the back of his leg with his foot.

'Well I think they are the prettiest unicorns I have ever seen.' said Ian laughing.

'I really hope you're drunk.' said Gilbert looking at Ian.

The lead Martian led them through to another room. Was Professor James's mind playing a jape on him or was the atmosphere growing increasingly tense. The number of Martians had him on edge as well. Why were there more now that they were trying to show them something?

The lead Martian stepped forward and pointed at Penny. Penny pointed at herself as if to verify the question. The creature nodded and Penny stepped forward but Professor James put his hand out and stopped her.

'It's ok Uncle James, I will be fine.'

'You are not going out of my sight.' said he gritting his teeth.

Penny walked up to the lead Martian, it felt her hair and played with it. Professor James felt his anger boiling at the sight of it touching his niece as he could not be sure of its intentions, if a man on the street had done that, he would have thumped them by now.

The creature let her be and a Martian that he had not seen before came from around a corner, it was different in colour, it was more green than blue yet not quite turquoise either. Professor James wondered whether it was a random phenomenon such as an albino.

The green creature produced a weird looking contraption, that looked like a delivery device or gun and there was green ooze dripping out of the end of it. The creature stepped toward Penny. Professor James looked at the lead Martian who held up his hand to stop him but the other one kept on walking towards Penny. He was about to step forward when two mighty hands grabbed his arms. Professor James saw Giles, Gilbert and Ian captured as well.

Professor James tried to struggle free but could not as the hands were so strong. His hunch had been right all along; something was amiss.

'Giles, get ready I am going to try and break free, they have flesh so I am trusting they feel pain. Whatever it takes to free Penny.'

'Damn right.' cried he.

'I'm in.' said Gilbert.

'*You will never succeed they have us now he-he-he.*' shrieked Ian.

Professor James stamped his foot on the foot of his captor and kicked back into the shin as hard he could, he did not feel bone but the effect was as desired and he was immediately released. He turned and punched it in the face which sent it staggering backwards, he followed up with a couple of jabs and the creature fell to the floor. The other Martians were stunned for a second and Giles took advantage using a similar tactic, he was quickly free but Gilbert failed and the two of them had to punch the Martian off him.

They were surrounded but Professor James wasted no time, he saw the abject fear in Penny's eyes and without hesitation pulled out his revolver, walked straight at the Martian with the delivery gun and pulled the trigger, a huge spray of blue blood came out of the side of its head. The Martian instantaneously dropped to the floor.

The Martian's reaction was one of surprise and amazement. Professor James could hear weird squeals coming from some of them, he pointed to Penny and beckoned her over. Giles had his revolver out as well and Gilbert had swung his rifle around.

Penny looked a little shocked but relieved as well. She walked toward her uncle with a slight tremble.

Professor James pointed the gun straight at the lead Martians head. The Martian held its hands up yet somehow Professor James sensed that it was not being sardonic or facetious.

The professor looked the Martian in the eyes.

'*You brought us all this way just to attack us and experiment on us, you fiend, I should shoot you dead.*'

The Martian shrugged its shoulders.

'*Confound you, you blasted Martian excrement.*' shouted Professor James firing his gun. The shot had the desired effect and scared back some of the Martians. Professor James made a run for the door and they all followed him, Gilbert had to grab Ian who tried to stay behind.

Professor James led with his gun sticking out and exited the way they had entered.

'No, no, I shall never leave them, never, they are our Gods, the ones to whom we bow.'

'Ian what is the matter with you? Tell me man, are you drunk?'

'Ha-ha-ha drunk on the miracle of science Professor, the stars have filled me with dream and wonder, now you wish to withhold all that I have discovered, no you rogue, even if it means death, mad, mad you say, he-he, the Quasars of the moon are full of childish sentiment.'

'Has he gone utterly mad?' said Giles.

'I don't know but we cannot leave him here.' said Gilbert.

'Quite.' remarked Professor James checking behind them. 'We have not got time to hang about.'

Professor James looked at his friend, his eyes were moving in strange orbits and he was unable to focus. Gilbert kept hold of his arm to stop him from wandering off.

'Come on we are nearly back at the chasm.' said Giles.

The party rushed out onto the small plateau that hugged the chasm.

'We came that way.' cried Penny pointing to the walkway with the bannister.

'*Get off me you confounded fool. I am fine.*' screamed Ian as he broke free from his grip and ran toward the edge.

'Ian, what the hell are you doing?' cried Professor James.

'Gilbert was already in flight.'

'I am fine you fools. I just need more of this.' said Ian pulling a strange piece of half-eaten fruit out of his pocket and taking a bite. Gilbert caught up with him, grabbed his hand and a struggle ensued.

'Give me that fruit damn it.'

'Never will you know what you don't possess.' cried Ian, the madness returning to his eyes.

Gilbert knocked the fruit out of his hands, Ian saw his beloved piece of fruit rolling toward the chasm and panicked, he kneed Gilbert in the groin, Gilbert doubled up and fell to the floor.

'*Stop Ian. Stop man.*' screamed Professor James.

Ian did not listen and seeing the fruit about to go over the precipice he dived with all his might, slid along the ground and went over the edge.

XVI The Illusion of Death

'*Noooooooooo!*' cried Professor James diving after him. He was just in time. Ian had grabbed a small jagged rock and was about to lose his grip when Professor James's torso flew over the edge and his hand thrust out toward him.

He grabbed his hand. Professor James could feel the immense weight of his friend trying to pull him over the edge.

'Hold on my friend, hold on.'

'Professor James. James, I can't, let me go.'

'You are talking rubbish man, it is the fruit, it has sent you mad. Why the bloody hell did you eat it for?'

'James, I want to die on Mars.'

'No, damn you, I don't care what you bloody well want, you are living and returning to Earth to claim your glory.'

'No I'm not.' said Ian letting go.

Professor James felt the weight of his friend slowly pulling him over the cliff as well.

'Giles.'

Professor James heard Giles diving to the Martian soil and felt his hand tightly grip his ankles. The Professor gripped his friend's wrist as hard he could but could still feel it slipping.

'Giles, rope damn it, rope.' he shouted.

'It is wrapped around me am I am laying on the bloody floor holding you.' said Giles feeling Penny and Gilbert desperately trying to pull them all back up by his legs.

Professor James felt his eyes moisten, his face red and contorted with determination.

'You have to live, you have to, you were right Ian, you were right all along.'

Professor James saw his old friend return to his eyes.

'About what?'

'The dinosaurs, they do have feathers, we found an island off Scotland that still has dinosaurs on it, I was saving it for when we got back, you were right my friend you will be laughed at no longer.'

Professor James saw a huge smile beam across Ian's face, he lost his grip and his beloved friend from university plunged. Professor James tried to get another hold and even though he thought it was as fast a reaction as a snake bite, it was still no match for gravity.

Penny screamed.

Professor James watched with a tear in his eye as his friend after shrinking considerably became a pattern of red on the purple jagged crystals below.

For a minute Professor James just lay there looking over the edge. It seemed tragically ironic that both people who had perished had done so by the very thing that had brought them there. He felt himself being pulled back over the edge.

'James he is gone. Nothing can be done, you know the rules, we grieve later.'

Professor James leapt to his feet.

'You what?' he said squaring up to Giles.

'Snap out of it man we have not got time.' replied he.

'No time at all actually.' said Gilbert.

The Martians had appeared and were running towards them.

Professor James lost in grief and rage shot dead three of them before purposefully pulling out a machete and hacking a fourth one to death.

'You want war with man. We'll give you a war.'

Another one appeared and held his hand out at them.

'Come on we must keep moving.' said Giles.

'Sorry old man. I lost myself for a second there.' said Professor James.

'Do not worry. I am well acquainted with your temper.'

'This is horrible, I just want to go home.' said Penny.

'We will darling I promise.' Professor James said grabbing her arm.

'Insects.' cried Gilbert.

'Blast, they are coming down the walkway we need another way out.' said Giles.

'There is another tunnel over there let us see where that goes.' said Professor James.

'We need to hide from the Martians and insects if possible. Let's run.'

Professor James led the charge and they ran toward the small narrow tunnel, as they got there an insect appeared and grew to full size but it did not reckon on Professor James's determination, he ducked and ran the machete straight through its body and kept on running, the others all jumped over the fatally wounded writhing creature.

Giles was close behind with Penny third and Gilbert in the rear ensuring Penny was not picked off.

They ran down the tunnel and onto a gantry.

'That's where we were before.' said Penny.

'Lower your voice.' said Giles.

They saw some Martians running out of the room they had previously been in and they were headed in the direction of the chasm.

'Reinforcements.' said Professor James.

'That means we are probably not heading in the wisest direction.' said Gilbert.

'I concur.' said Giles.

'No time to debate, the decision has been made, follow me.' said Professor James.

They ran across the intersection and into the next corridor then into a room that turned out to be another cavern. Professor James stopped. He looked around and could not see a single Martian.

'It doesn't make sense does it Giles?'

'No, it is too quiet.'

'What are those things down there?' said Penny.

They all looked down into the cavern, there was an industrial factory or at least that is what it looked like and rows of the green meteorite.

'As you all know I am not particular believer in coincidence.' said Professor James.

'I fail to follow squire, where is the coincidence?'

'Look at the lumps of green rock Gilbert.'

'That huge chute at the end with the mighty machine attached to it looks perfectly capable of delivering missiles to Earth.' said Giles.

'They are targeting Earth.' said Professor James.

'It appears so.' said Giles.

'More than appears I would say By Jove.' said Gilbert.

'I am not so sure. There is something that does not add up here.'

'Penny, nothing has added up since the second we set foot on this planet.'

'I know that Uncle but it still does not sit right with me albeit I will confess that it does seem the way you see.'

'Perhaps we should see what else we can find if humanity is depending on it.' said Gilbert.

Professor James turned around to Giles, Gilbert and Penny. They all nodded.

They continued on and Professor James realised that an offshoot that they had passed led back into the room that they had come from originally. He was tempted to go back and examine the dead Martian to see what he could learn. He decided that they had already tempted fate enough that day.

How could he have been so stupid? They should have just stayed in the first meadow, documented everything and returned to the craft. His scientific brain fought against his emotion, you are a scientist and you explore, that is what you are supposed to do. Professor James wondered how many more faces would haunt him over the years.

The expeditioners passed through the cavern and entered another one, this one had vehicles in it, rows and rows of weird looking ships, it looked like they had thrusters but how the technology worked was impossible to tell. The first thing other than the ships that Professor James noticed was that they were heavily guarded by the large insects.

'We need to be silent and hug this wall as there is an army of insects down there.' said Professor James.

'So I see.' said Giles.

'I think we should call them beetles as that is more what they look like.' said Penny.

'Ok Penny, there is an army of beetles down there.' said Professor James giving her a sharp look.

'It is the first time we have seen any sense of military organisation and that is rather odd considering the amount of ground we have covered.' said Giles.

'We have obviously got right into the heart of their civilisation.' said Gilbert nearly tripping over as he walked too close to the wall.

The party stopped to take another look at the space crafts below.

'They must have wanted to lure us in to the centre but for the life of me I cannot fathom why. They have had endless opportunities to surround us, kidnap us or even kill us so why all the laborious circumnavigating?' said Professor James checking that his gun was loaded.

'There is a lot that does not make sense and that is what worries me. These fiends may well have invasion on their minds.' said Giles.

'I think when we get home we should draw some kind of time line of events and map out exactly what we encountered and where, whether there was any design in it or what was missing. When looking for clues people always look for what is there and forget what is missing.'

'Quite.' said Professor James looking at Gilbert with a smile. 'You remember that young lady, Gilbert is correct you should always think of what is missing as well as what you can see, like right now for example.'

'Right now?' asked Penny.

'We have stopped above their most precious commodity and yet we are able to stand here and have a conversation, there are no guards or beetles anywhere up here and we escaped at this level as well, why?' said Professor James.

There was a momentary silence.

'We must look at the evidence in front of us, they have the capability of firing missiles at Earth and have successfully done so little knowing that we would come to Mars first. Now we know they have an invasion fleet they must be planning to fire many missiles at Earth.'

'But they did not inflict any real damage?' said Gilbert cautiously leaning over the railing to get a closer look.

'Fuel. What if they need the rocks for fuel and energy it would make sense to ply your battlefield with the required resources before you land, especially if it is a foreign planet.' said Penny.

'That would hold.' said Giles 'and let us not forget all the scenes of Earth we saw was England, the meteor landed in England and not that far from London either, relatively speaking.'

'That makes sense as a military plan.' said Professor James.

'What about the plants?' said Gilbert.

'An accident. The plant was tiny and well-hidden I doubt it was meant to be on there.' said Penny.

'Then why not take the green crystal on their ships then?' said Gilbert.

'Think of all the space and weight. If were not for Ian's love of milk,' there was a brief pause at the mention of Ian's name but Professor James remembering the cardinal rule of exploration carried on, 'it would have been nothing more than another lump of rock for a museum and when more started to land we would assume it was a devastating meteor shower.'

'It all makes perfect sense and is a fairly ingenious invasion plan, we would not have had a clue.' said Giles.

'Invasion.' said Professor James.

'What if they did not know they need oxygen on Earth?' said Giles.

'Good God they do now! They must have seen us using their plants in our suits.' cried Gilbert.

They all looked at each other.

'If that is true they could bring any timetable forward and launch an invasion immediately.' said Professor James.

'What have we done?' said Giles.

'Something still does not add up?' said Penny looking through her sketchbook.

'Penny, there is no other logical explanation.' said Gilbert. 'What do we do now Professor James?'

'We need to get straight back to Earth and warn the populous. Penny, will you stop doodling in your bloody journal and pay attention please?'

'Sorry, I was just trying to figure something out.'

'Well please pay attention it is most irksome.'

'She's alright.'

'Stop sticking up for her Giles now is not the bloody time.'

Giles shrugged his shoulders and looked at Penny.

'I do think we should try and uncover whatever information we can. When we leave let us be as vigilant as possible for any intel, there may be a machine or weapon we can learn from or take back with us.'

'Yes, that information would be of great merit.' said Giles. 'Do you think we should try and sneak down and take a look at one of the ships?'

'There are too many guards.' said Gilbert.

'We have lost too many people already today. I could not bear to lose anyone else.' said Penny finally paying attention to the conversation.

'Agreed although I think we should go back down this corridor as you can access the room where they attacked Penny. If we are lucky we might be able to see exactly what they planned.' said Professor James.

'Dissection probably.' said Gilbert.

'Have to say not very sporting, playing the perfect host and then attacking us.' said Giles.

'That is why they wanted us to eat the fruit.' said Professor James instantly seeing Ian falling to his death again in his mind.

'That way we would put up no resistance.' said Giles.

'Then they could experiment and probe to their hearts content.' added Gilbert.

Professor James looked at Penny and noticed that concern was painted across her face like a garish sign for a new tonic shop.

'Let us not dawdle, we have plenty to do and I do not know how long it will be before we are discovered. I want a quick look in that room.'

'Let us all go.' said Penny.

There were nods of approval and Professor James led them to the back entrance corridor. He pulled out his revolver and instructed the others to wait there, they were only to come if he called them.

He slunk down the corridor with his gun out looking only in the direction that the barrel was pointed as someone had once taught him to do. Professor James entertained a fleeting thought that he would not have minded a stint in the military and then could not help but snigger to himself that his life was exciting enough. His guess was accurate, it was the room that they were all in before their break for freedom and he sensed that he was not alone. Professor James moved silently with his gun still drawn hoping that he may be able to spare one of the Martians if it was alone. The room was empty and he realised that the alien that tried to stab Penny must have taken this exact route. The weird gun was gone but the body was still there. He froze.

The sense of someone with him was overwhelming, he pretended to creep forward and without warning spun on his heels and went to pull the trigger.

XVII A Priceless Find

'*Penelope Bedford, what the hell do you think you're doing?* I nearly shot you.'

'Sorry, I could not help it.'

'You stupid, stupid, girl you do as your bloody well told when you're on expedition with me.'

'Yes Uncle James.'

'Don't yes uncle me Penny; I nearly shot you dead!'

Penny turned on her puppy dog eyes. Professor James stood there looking at her determined it was not going to work.

'We have not got time for this right now, you are nineteen not eight but it seems you have not matured enough yet. We will discuss your behaviour at a future date but I would not get excited about the prospect of joining me again.'

'I sincerely apologise, I didn't mean to make you angry, I just wanted to get a look at the dead alien.'

Penny rushed over to examine it.

'Quick then as you're here.' said Professor James reminding himself that it was his niece that had got him so angry. He returned his focus to the environment.

'They have teeth, lungs and eyes but the fundamental difference is the skin, it does not feel or look like human tissue.'

'Damn it there is nothing here and we cannot get these blasted screens to work.' said Professor James struggling with the weird control panel. Professor James heard footsteps and familiar guttural noises.

'They're coming; quick Penny.'

Penny looked up and heard them too but just as she was about to get up she spied something under one of the tables.

'What is that?'

'I don't care Penny. Let's go now.'

'Just one second.' said Penny diving under the table, retrieving the object and running past her uncle and down the corridor, Professor James was in hot pursuit and within seconds they were back with the others.

'Run, they are coming, try and get beyond the spaceships to see what we can find.'

A quick glance behind him and Professor James, Giles, Penny and Gilbert were running along as if they were some children off on an adventure, in another circumstance the scene might have been amusing. Once again they got clear of the meteorite loading bay and were back in the hangar with all the space craft.

Up ahead there was a junction, one path led straight on into another cavern whilst the other took a left across the hangar running over the spaceships and insects and then into another hangar. Professor James stopped they were all gasping for breath.

Giles looked back down the way they had come. 'They must not have heard us.'

'Damn lucky, I am sure they entered the room the second I left it.' said Professor James.

'I think lucky is the right word.' said Giles 'Let us go straight on. That direction has served us well so far.'

'I agree.' said Penny.

'Perhaps but what is of concern to me is that we are heading further in the wrong direction. I have been keeping it in the back of my mind and albeit we have been spun around a few times I am convinced that this is not the way back to the Mad Professor.'

'My deductions are the same.'

'I'm glad about that Giles you're supposed to be the intrepid sailor and explorer.' said Professor James.

'Despite my compass not working due to the skewed magnetic fields of this planet I have been keeping a keen eye on our geographic position and I also think we are heading in totally the wrong direction.'

'Well let us see what is there. Look how much we have discovered so far.' said Penny adjusting her bag around her shoulder.

'Ok let us see what is in the next section, then I favour going across to our left, it is risky I know but our luck is a little too incredible for me so far and the nearer we get to the space ship the more reassured I will be.'

'I think you speak for all of us there Professor.' said Gilbert.

'Let us press on and keep your guns drawn.' said Professor James looking at the cavern wall that separated them from the next section.

They crept through like a gang of robbers sneaking through the rear entrance of an unsuspecting bank.

'That is the fruit they offered us.' cried Penny.

'The bastards, they are going to try and send us all mad, then round us up and pick us off.' said Gilbert.

'Let's keep moving.' said Giles.

'No Giles, there is nothing but fruit here and we are heading in the wrong direction.' said Professor James.

'And?'

'I don't know Giles let us say it is a hunch.'

'I like hunches.' said Giles.

'A hunch it is then.' said Gilbert.

'I have a hunch my niece has a borderline unhealthy obsession with that blasted notebook, if we stop for thirty seconds her head is inside it.'

'One should always record every detail.' replied Penny.

'Well keep your wits about you young lady.' said Giles.

Penny looked up at Giles and smiled.

'She gets her insolence from you, you know.' said Giles crossing his arms and looking at Professor James.

'I would be negative on that one.' replied he.

'I'm afraid she does. She looked just like you then.' said Gilbert.

Penny laughed.

'You two can bugger off and stop corrupting my niece.' said Professor James marching back toward the junction.

They all followed, Giles and Penny were sniggering along the way which only infuriated Professor James more.

They got back to the junction and Professor James stopped dead, turned around and put his finger to his lips and pointed below. The spaceships were still protected by insects. They walked across the gantry as quietly as possible, luck was on their side as the metal was unlike anything on Earth and their feet made little noise. Professor James thought that the silence of the metal had probably been their saviour on numerous occasions.

Glancing down they could see most of the insects were stationed by machines. Professor James was in no doubt that these creatures were nothing short of centurions. They had the forethought to guard their ships yet they had been allowed to run around freely, why? Again that feeling of unease settled in his stomach like when you eat something and intuition tells you it was not right and you are to be ill. What if the Martians wanted to watch them and study their habits under stress, their ingenuity skills as they try to escape. The best way to defeat your enemy is to know him inside out, stalk him, watch him and control his every movement without him knowing it.

Professor James hated the feeling like this and he had to swallow his anger, rationality was the only way out, everybody makes mistakes and it only takes one for the tables to be turned. Professor James briefly wondered where that saying had come from and then he remembered his Sunday school teacher telling the story of Jesus turning the tables in the synagogues and continued satisfied that this was its source.

No one dared speak on the gantry, it was long and despite being at the back of the cavern was exposed, it would only take one of the insects to look up in the right direction and notice them. Professor James walked fast but with a calm pace and luckily there was some light background noise coming from below. He could not detect the source of the humming and he wondered whether the ships were powering up.

They were two thirds across when Penny whispered loudly.

'There is a commotion.'

Professor James snapped his head in the direction where Penny was pointing. An insect had stepped out of position and it seemed to be looking at them, one of its huge antler sabres pointed in their direction, the other insects turned and looked up.

'*Run.*' shouted Professor James.

They all ran into the next cavern.

'Just as I thought.' said Professor James. 'These purple crystals are some sort of fuel like the green ones that we used.'

'We need to keep moving they will be on us very soon.' said Giles.

'They have not appeared in this cavern which means there is no connection yet. Can you see a way down?' said Professor James.

'Not the greatest design is it? You would think there would be more stairs.' said Penny.

'I think the point is to get across the caverns not through them.' said Gilbert.

'We should stay up here Uncle James.' said Penny. 'The creatures are on a different level to us.'

'That is exactly my point. With luck they will all come up here and try to get us but what if we can get down there. Come on.'

They followed Professor James as he ran down the gantry and to a section nearing the wall. 'Look at the rocks they are staggered I think we should be able to climb down them safely.'

'It is a long way down and if we fall we will be seriously injured.' said Penny.

'That's why we can't fall. You should be the best climber out of us all Penny.'

'Giles keep guard and come last, I will go first then Penny, then Gilbert.'

'Righto.' said Giles.

Professor James climbed over the weird feeling balcony and lowered himself down onto a rock. The rocks of Mars felt similar to that of Earth but a little rougher and the Martian dust was thick and acrid but it seemed to their advantage acting like climber's chalk. Without warning his foot gave way and he heard Penny gasp, Professor James easily grabbed the side of another rock and steadied himself, he thought about the rope but they did not have time. It took Professor James another couple of minutes but he was quickly down to the cavern floor despite the height.

He shouted for Penny and she made it an easier job than him, at one point Professor James told her to slow down for fear that she would slip and fall as he nearly did. Gilbert was the only one who struggled but they were soon all reunited on the cavern floor.

Professor James was worried as he was expecting a marauding army of killer insects to enter their cavern at any second. He looked at where they were, it was a huge dump of purple crystals that looked like they had been mined.

Professor James also noted that there were no plants in there and yet they were not having breathing problems, he accounted for it by way of the sheer volume of the other plants elsewhere, after all Earth had deserts yet oxygen was everywhere.

Professor James had his revolver out and thought to recheck that the chamber was full and the hammer pulled back. It was then he realised that even with all the ammo they had it was not enough to fight a war and the revolvers and rifles were not the fastest things to reload. He looked at all the shards of purple crystal and wondered how they might be used. He walked over and picked one up.

'What are you thinking Uncle James?' said Penny.

'We need an advantage as we are preposterously outnumbered.'

'A weapon you mean?'

'Yes Gilbert.' said Professor James holding the grapefruit sized rock up to his eye so he could examine it.

'Why don't we do an experiment?' said Gilbert.

'What do you mean?' replied Professor James.

'We have the dynamo that produces electric so we can start the ship.' said Gilbert.

'Blast, Ian had it last.'

'No he didn't.' said Giles appearing from the rockface. 'I took it off him earlier, I was not sure about him keeping it safe.'

'Quick, we have not got time to waste.'

'No we haven't.' said Penny. 'Up on the gantry.'

Professor James looked up and saw a hoard of beetles come pouring through.

'Quick Giles run a charge through it.'

Giles turned the handle as fast he could, sparks started flying and then a brief but small bolt of electricity passed through the receptors, he turned it ever more furiously until the blue bolt was consistent.

'Be careful.' said Penny.

'Yes, better put it on the floor and stand back everyone just in case.'

Professor James placed it on the floor, Giles bent down and held the charge to it, immediately there was a reaction and the crystal shone as if there was a nucleus inside of it. Giles stepped back.

'Well at least there was a reaction.' said Giles.

'The electricity is reacting with it.' said Penny.

'Quite.' said Professor James watching as the blue streaks of lightning were caressing and dancing around the crystal.

'The pattern is increasing and the streaks are getting faster.' said Giles.

'Well let us use logic, the crystal must be holding the charge and magnifying, storing and creating energy.' said Gilbert.

'So what happens when it can hold no more energy?' said Penny.

Professor James and Giles looked at each other. Professor James leapt forward grabbed the crystal and threw it up on to the gantry near where a couple of insects were still watching, just as it landed there was an almighty explosion, debris and dust rained down.

'Right let's move everybody. Weapons ready to fire that includes you Penny. Giles you hold the dynamo I will light them and throw. Now everybody as quick as you can, grab some crystals, you saw how powerful that was so get different sizes.'

'Bloody hell it has blown half the wall away.' said Giles.

As the dust cleared Professor James saw there was a gaping hole in the wall, the cavern was higher than St Paul's Cathedral and yet just a grapefruit size piece did that, if it was a three bedroom house there would have been nothing left standing.

'Get mainly smaller pieces.' added Giles. 'Just one grapefruit sized one each.'

Penny picked a large one up. 'They're so light.' she squealed.

'They're coming through the hole in the wall.' said Giles holstering his revolver, swinging his rifle down over his shoulder and switching to a kneeling position before letting off a shot, an insect fell then another and another and finally a fourth. Professor James grabbed some small crystals and a couple of large ones as well.'

'I have filled my satchel.' said Penny.

'Excellent, everyone do the same and as much as you can, quick. You too Giles they have stopped coming through.'

'They are quick learners.' replied Giles.

'Yes they are, we need to keep the element of surprise and run for our ship, it is the only hope we have, with these hopefully they will give us safe passage once they see the power we possess.'

'*Watch out.*' screamed Penny.

XVIII The Professor's Revenge

Professor James turned and let out two volleys with his revolver, the approaching beetles fell and so did the two behind them, three more as Gilbert and Penny opened up. Giles lit a crystal and threw it toward the archway in the corner of the room that they had started to pour through. There was a huge explosion and high-pitched squealing not dissimilar to a pig being slaughtered.

'What a horrible sound.' cried Penny.

'Death never sounds pleasant.' said Professor James.

'Good throw.' said Giles.

'Not really.' said Gilbert. 'You've blocked off our escape.'

'Confound it I never thought of that.' said Professor James looking at the pile of rubble where the entrance had been.

'Never mind, I would rather go this way there is something I need to do. Follow me.'

'We are not going back up the rock face are we?' said Gilbert.

'Not that one.' replied Giles seeing where Professor James had in mind.

They all jogged over the vast space to the collection of fallen boulders that had once been the wall. Professor James did not speak just started climbing.

'Come on quick, we can climb up to the broken gantry.' said Professor James.

His solid calf muscles flexed as he strode up the huge rocks, he could feel the ache already but he rather enjoyed it as he was used to working out and had decided to keep fit from a young age, many people had commented how he was not like a usual scientist. He looked behind to see the others following, the only thing concerning him was that the other side could be teeming with beetles.

Professor James stopped a few metres down from the top and motioned for Giles to join him but for the others to stay put. Professor James knelt down, cocked his gun, crept to the top, carefully lifted his head over and quickly ducked as a black sabre nearly decapitated him. He shot the thing in its face, yellow ooze flew out and spattered over Professor James, he had no time to be disgusted and emptied the gun into the remaining insects. Giles went to light a crystal.

'No, they are retreating.'

'It worries me Giles that they are such quick learners we need to watch out for traps I think.'

'Agree completely my old friend, let's just keep going, I have a surprise for them.'

Professor James stepped down a couple of rocks, then ran back up and jumped to reach the fallen metal, he grabbed the pole, pulled himself up and managed to climb back onto the gantry.

'Is it safe?' said Penny.

'It is stable enough; now move it.' said Professor James. 'Gilbert, behind you.'

Gilbert turned around and saw more beetles approaching the rock face they were on.

'Confound them they have found a way through.' cried he putting away his gun and pulling out a rifle which pleased

Professor James as Gilbert was a bad shot with a rifle but a worse shot with a revolver.

Giles pulled himself up easily as he was used to it and had climbed the rope nets of a ship many times, even in the fiercest of storms.

Penny could not pull herself up so Giles lowered the rope for her, Gilbert having successfully driven back the tempted trespassers got most of the way but needed help to get up, over and on to the gantry.

'*Come on.*' cried Professor James running down the gantry and turning left.

'Where the hell are we going?' said Giles.

'Just follow me.' replied he walking into the cavern with all the fruit in.

'What are you up to professor?' asked Gilbert.

'In war what is it that you always aim to do?'

'That is a bit cryptic Professor.' said Penny 'Defeat the enemy?'

'Yes but how?'

'Kill them?' said Gilbert.

'I was thinking more cut off their supply lines.' replied Professor James pulling out a huge lump of crystal.

'Blow the bloody planet up let alone their supplies.' said Giles.

'I have another one for next door.' replied Professor James.

'The ships, of course, without them they cannot attack Earth.' cried Gilbert.

'Quite.' said Professor James holding the rock toward Giles who lit it with electricity as soon as he saw the first blue flash, Professor James threw it as hard as he could into the middle of the cavern.

They sprinted out of the room and into the other. There was a huge explosion so loud they were all certain they would never hear again, they were thrown to the floor violently and Penny felt blood running down her leg.

The gantry shook and small rocks began to fall from the ceiling. Professor James got to his feet, the gantry shook again as another quake hit from the after-effects of the explosion, Professor James pulled out another huge crystal.

'Are you mad?' cried Gilbert.

'The transport is in the hangar we cannot take any chances, even if we die, we must destroy it otherwise our world is doomed. But we do need to make sure Penny gets home.' said Professor James looking at his niece. 'Penny your leg!' he said throwing the huge rock at Giles who only just managed to catch it.

'Is it ok?' he said bending down. 'Is it broken?'

'I do not believe so. I can move it but it is as sore as hell.'

'I need to see the wound.' said Professor James pulling out a clean handkerchief and wiping away the blood. 'You have just tore up your knee, largely superficial I suspect, try and push through it we can rest later and the pain will subside soon. Come on, I will help you to your feet.'

Penny got up, flexed her knee and limped around some. 'Yes, you are right uncle.'

They raced back into the previous cavern where the ships were. Professor James took the huge chunk of crystal from Giles and watched the charge go through it, he saw Giles's face glow a weird purple as the crystal ignited. Professor James threw it through the air.

Penny started running first but they all joined her into the dead Martian room, they continued through and back into the passage the way they had come, as they exited the room the explosion hit. All four of them were sent crashing to the floor as the ground itself shook and writhed. The ceiling in the room behind them caved in engulfing them in a plume of dust. They covered their faces as best they could.

Professor James jumped up and yanked Penny up by her arm. 'We have to go now.'

They kept on running, the ground shook again but they managed to stay on their feet but rocks were starting to fall, another two explosions in quick succession and they saw flames leaping through cracks of fallen rocks.

It was not long before they came to the opening with the giant chasm where Ian had lost his life.

'Stop.' said Professor James.

'But you just said we should not man.'

'Sorry Gilbert there is something I must do.'

Explosions were still rumbling in the distance Professor James as calm as the River Fleet on a hot July day walked over, looked down into the chasm and saw the bright red mark spattered on an ocean of purple crystal that was once his old university friend.

'Someone give me a large crystal, the largest you have please.' said he.

Penny and Giles both pulled huge stones out. Penny's was the largest so Professor James took hers.

'Giles?' said he.

'What are you playing at?'

'*Just light the damned thing will you.*' snapped Professor James.

Giles rolled his eyes and ignited it. Professor James stood at the precipice of the opening and gently threw it aiming right at the remains of his friend.

'Have your revenge my old friend.' said he.

'*You fool.*' cried Gilbert you will blow the whole planet in half.

Each one of them was aware the explosion would be huge. They sprinted across the gantry that went over the chasm, Giles was leading the way when Penny ran past him and screamed as she went over the edge. The weight was heavy and solid but his muscles were prepared for the shock and his grip held firm, Giles pulled with his all might letting out a guttural groan as he did so but Penny was safe and back on the gantry.

'What happened?'

'A huge rock has come down and smashed the gantry I just caught it out of the corner of my eye but smart old Penny here thought she would overtake me.'

'Thank you Giles.' said Penny hugging him.

'Not now Penny we're-'

They were interrupted as Professor Ian Oakley's remains exploded with the force of a volcano and they grabbed onto the rail. Before anyone could protest Professor James launched himself over the gap on to the other side, he managed to catch the railing and pull himself up, fire erupted from the pit where Ian had fallen.

'Use the rope quickly.' yelled Professor James.

Using teamwork they used the rope to ensure they all made the jump.

As soon as they were all across they ran across the rest of the gantry as more explosions rocked them. The ground was rumbling and shaking and large rocks were starting to fall from the ceiling.

'I fear we have set off a chain reaction,' said Gilbert.

There was a huge quake and they dived to the ground as dust enveloped them. Professor James got up and saw they were unrecognisable as they were covered in Martian dust, he had his shirt over his nose and mouth and saw that the whole cavern had fallen in. His nose was tingling and he could not smell for the dust, it was making his eyes water and a little sore, he put it to the back of his mind they had to get out as fast as possible.

'I believe we have Gilbert,' said he.

'Penny and Gilbert got up coughing; Gilbert with particular violence. They reached for their beer bottles, swilled their mouths and then spat it out as if they were chewing tobacco.

Professor James smiled as he was confident that they had stopped their operation but whether Earth would be safe he did not know.

'I think that has put a stop to them.' said Professor James.

'What makes you think that?' said Gilbert still spluttering.

'Because we have destroyed their food, their fuel and their transport, that is why Gilbert. You haven't been eating that fruit as well have you?'

'No I have not and I would appreciate it if you would not be so insolent.'

'Disrespectful would be more the word but forgive my sarcasm. What are you trying to convey to me?'

'What if the whole planet is covered in bases like this?'

'That is a possibility but let us just say that I am living in blind faith for now.'

'So am I.' said Giles.

Penny remained silent but was looking in her notebook.

'Let us continue, this is not the place to stand and debate, more of this structure may collapse yet.'

'I agree.' said Giles. 'Let us get back to the ... I have just realised we still have to go back through the city and up that infernal staircase which will be a lot harder than it was coming down, then across the chasm through all the meadows and back to our suits and even then it is still quite a way to the exit.'

'I know and even though the extra energy these super oxygenated plants are giving us I am still feeling tired.' said Professor James.

'So am I. It is bizarre it is like my brain is not that tired but my physical body is screaming something at me and it is as if I do not understand.' said Giles.

'You mentioned that earlier on Professor James, an astute observation, just as you had predicted it is affecting us without our knowing.' said Gilbert.

The party marched on swiftly, there were quakes and tremors and albeit he did not mention it because of Penny, Professor James was gravely concerned the whole structure would come down. The team continued without encountering any beetles or Martians. Professor James kept on reminding himself that there could be a trap.

Onward they marched and were soon back at the temple with the pillars. Professor James halted and they all stopped behind him.

'Something is not right.' said he.

'I was thinking the same thing.' said Gilbert.

'How is your leg Penny?'

'It is fine thank you Uncle James.'

'Weapons out I think from here on.' said Professor James pulling out his gun and walking forward.

As they came toward the great doors that led out on to the steps and the city beyond Professor James motioned for Giles to go to the other side of the doorway and indicated for Penny and Gilbert to stay put. Gilbert stood back and set up a firing stance with the rifle. Professor James was pleased with the forethought. Penny was holding the revolver, it looked loose in her hand and he made a note to ensure that he got her used to handling a gun when they returned to Earth.

Professor James craned his head around the corner of the doorway and immediately pulled it back in.

'What is the matter with you?' cried Giles.

'Take a look, there is not much point in running or even hiding I would say.' replied he.

Giles put his head around the corner and came back with the same expression of horror that Professor James had.

'What is wrong? Are we surrounded or something.' said Gilbert.

'Your intuition serves you correctly dear boy.' said Professor James.

'Surrounded is an understatement. Half the bloody planet is waiting for us.' added Giles.

'What do we do?' said Penny heading over to have a look.

Gilbert followed.

'Quite a predicament we have found ourselves in. Any ideas?' said Gilbert.

'We have lost the element of surprise and I would think the reason our encounters have been so minimal is because they knew we would have to pass this point. From a battle perspective I find it hard to imagine that this is not their last stand.'

'We have the Martian grenades Giles?'

'That maybe Gilbert but how many large ones do we have.'

'A couple of really big ones.' replied Gilbert.

Penny showed Gilbert her bag.

'Quite a few medium sized ones and considering just how powerful they are we could take out half the city with the large ones alone.'

'Do we have any small ones like really small strawberry or a small cox apple size?' said Professor James.

'Yes, I picked some small ones so that I would have more in my bag and the thought also occurred to me it would be advantageous to have just enough power if we need it rather than complete overkill.'

'I have a plan. Pass it to me Penny and well done.'

Penny did as she was told.

'Giles, when I say I want you to ignite it.'

'Consider it done.' replied he.

Professor James stepped out of the doorway and the others slowly followed, everybody had their weapons drawn apart from Professor James.

The first thing that Professor James noticed was a handful of Martians riding the giant beetles just like a cavalry position on a battlefield. The three lead Martians all sat abreast beetles. It was most disconcerting like a weird dream one has after reading the history of mediaeval battles only to discover a beetle in your garden later that afternoon, the two memories forming in your sleep and mixing with your imagination like a witch's brew.

There was a giant rumble, the ground shook tremendously and there was the loudest crash Professor James had ever heard, he thought that must have been what

Mount Vesuvius sounded like when it exploded and buried Pompeii.

A huge cloud of dust enveloped them.

'Don't run.' Professor James shouted.

Professor James figured the last of the infrastructure had just collapsed. He took a deep breath and stepped down a couple of steps. The lead Martian held up his hand. Professor James stood there staring at him, one of the Martians started to walk up the stairs and Professor James pulled out his revolver, clicked back the hammer and pointed it at him. The Martian looked at its leader and then retreated.

Professor James turned and looked at Giles to ensure he was right behind him. Penny and Giles were still at the top of the steps. He held up the small purple crystal between his thumb and index finger as if showing off a diamond.

He walked over to one side well clear of everybody and held up his hand. The Martians stood there watching, the beetles moved a little as if restless, they were acting almost like horses and a brief flash of horses riding beetles came into Professor James's mind. He got Giles to show them the dynamo then took the crystal and ignited it, he placed it on the floor and ran back to the centre of the stairs and stood there looking at the army of Martians steadfast as if daring them to counter.

A large explosion, larger than Professor James had intended, had the crowd cowering. The left-hand flank scattered but the rest stayed put and the leader made a very loud noise which Professor James took to be a command. As they started regrouping and falling back into position Professor James pointed at the crater in the ground, held up an index finger and motioned for Gilbert and Penny to come down the steps and stand behind him. Professor James turned around and took a huge crystal out of his bag and held it up high in the air. Then he lowered it toward the pulsing blue spark.

The lead Martian made a noise which whilst loud sounded more like a plea. Professor James threw the rock to

Gilbert and motioned with his hands for them all to get out of the way. The lead Martian nodded and Professor James considered that they were mastering body language exceedingly quick, he thought that if they had not have been hostile, he could have attempted to teach them sign language.

Giles had charged the dynamo so much that it was holding its charge as they slowly walked down the steps. The Martians and beetles cleared the way and the party slowly walked down to the bottom. Professor James stopped opposite the lead Martian and looked it straight in the eyes.

'If any of you ever come to Earth, I shall come back up here and kill you all.'

The creature showed no emotion but Professor James sensed that it understood that it was a threat.

The Martian waved them away and the garrisons and spectators all stepped further back.

'Keep that charge near this rock Giles in case they try anything. As soon as it is lit they will know to run.'

'So will we.' said Giles with a smile.

'We would probably be killed as well but let us hope they do not figure that out.'

They walked slowly eyeing up the strange creatures, they all had their hand on the trigger, even Penny was ready to fire and kept pointing the gun to either side. After a while they quickened their pace realising that they were going to obey the instructions from the front.

They eventually got back to the staircase, there were beetles and Martians stationed on every landing. Giles was complaining as his arms were aching and he kept on having to charge the dynamo but Professor James silenced him as he was having to carry the crystal and it was weighing on him too. They were all getting uncomfortable walking with their guns drawn and constantly being in a state of high alert was exhausting, they were starting to feel it more and more. Penny grabbed one of her spare leaves with her hands and pushed it to her mouth and nose to reinvigorate herself. It

197

worked but apparently not as good as before and she knew that her body must be extremely tired. It was time to go home, they all knew and it appeared that they would be allowed to.

The stairs were taking its toll on their calves and lungs as they walked up the endless staircase past many layers of well-guarded abodes. It had all seemed so exciting and new with energy abounding but now they were fatigued, hungry, thirsty and mentally worn down.

Eventually they got to the top of the staircase and Professor James lit the huge crystal and threw it over.

XIX A Daunting Prospect

'*Noooo!*' screamed Penny '*Why did you do that? Why?*'
'*Run, damn you child.*' cried Professor James.

The explosion ripped through the cavern a huge piece of debris just missed Gilbert and a large stone dashed against Professor James's arm heavily bruising and cutting it. His shirt was ripped and blood was pouring down his arm but it appeared to be just a nasty gash and he could still move it. Squeals and cries of anguish filled the air and Penny tried to block them out, she threw a wild look of hatred at her uncle for a second.

She breathed out just as her uncle yanked her arm and dragged her forward, she heard the staircase collapse and the roof coming down as they finally came out of the very outer building in the canyon.

They continued their journey home and seeing that no one was there they crossed the canyon in silence each with their own reflections and opinions on their adventure.

Professor James had so many questions that he tried to stop asking but found that he could not, just like any scientist he was becoming obsessed with them but it was further exhausting him as was the grief. He had lost two friends, it was very hard for him to think of Ian. Professor James was both sad and vexed at the bittersweet end of his life.

Humiliated and bullied Ian had at last found vindication only to die before the world realised it. He looked at his niece and wondered what damage all this would have upon Penny and cursed himself for bringing her. She was forced to grow up since the death of her mother but maybe he had taken it too far.

They journeyed down the other side of the slope and out by the river they saw Martians in the field watching them as they descended.

Professor James remained silent just clicking back the hammer of his revolver he was too tired to argue.

'Get ready to fire and make sure you have full rounds, keep the dynamo charged and we will use small ones to keep them away.' said Professor James.

They got to the bottom and the Martians surrounded them. Professor James pointed his gun at the one right in front of him, the creature fell on to all fours, the others did the same and then lowered their front legs.

'What are they doing?' said Gilbert.

'Begging.' replied Professor James walking forward and putting the gun against one of their heads.

'Remember this mercy.' said he uncocking the hammer and pulling the trigger away. The creature moved its head in some kind of nodding gesture, Professor James took it to mean thank you.

'Why did you not kill it? It would have killed us.'

'Because Gilbert we are scientists and explorers not genocidal maniacs, we should not have killed anyone but Earth was at risk, we have just destroyed an entire city and killed thousands if not hundreds of thousands but I am not going to be the one responsible for wiping out a species. They will think twice about visiting Earth now of that I am certain.'

'I agree it has been a nasty business but up to now a necessary one.' said Giles.

'I just want to go home.' said Penny with tears running down her face.

'We will now darling I promise.' said Professor James hugging her. She embraced him. 'I warned you it was not always pretty out in the field you should not have come.'

'I should have and I am coming on your next adventure I assure you.'

'We will talk about that later.' said he.

They walked back through the meadow and at last started to relax a little, they stopped for some food and refreshment, their leg muscles immediately reacted to the rest and they enjoyed every second that they sat. Professor James was convinced it was the last they had seen of the Martians. The team forced themselves to continue on until at last they saw the small cliff with the track leading down where they had first encountered all the alien wildlife.

So tired were they that they nearly forgot they had suits to collect. They got to the edge and looked for the plants where they had stashed the suits, they were all there. Professor James, Penny, Gilbert and Giles all put their suits on and this gave them a much needed boost of adrenaline and super oxygen as they sealed their helmets in place.

After a final walk, at last they were outside, the Martian red dust was swirling and blowing but they could still see the trail, they walked single file back towards their ship in silence. They got back and found it with its nose still sticking up just as they had landed. More sand had settled around it so they dug it out to ensure ignition.

Professor James and Giles handed the shovels back to Penny who was in the craft. Gilbert had already taken his seat and Giles got in after leaving his shovel stuck in the sand. Professor James got the shovel and went to pass it to Penny, he saw Penny's eyes open wide with fear.

'*Watch out.*' she cried.

Professor James saw in the reflection of her helmet a Martian reaching his hand toward him but it was not a Martian for it was wearing one of their suits. Professor James seeing that the hand was almost upon him threw the shovel, grabbed a lump hammer and swung it full force toward the faceplate he heard a deep warbled and guttural cry 'Wait!'

It was too late the face plate smashed and the Martian's eyes opened wide with terror, then started expanding out of its head, as did its tongue and face. Professor James kicked it, the Martian stumbled back, gave him one last look and then literally exploded. He wiped the blood off his faceplate, got on board and then shut the door.

'Get us out of here now Giles.'

Giles started the ignition and Professor James having successfully closed the door on the first go leapt into the seat and grabbed the controls, he ripped the helmet off his head and was relieved that he could still breathe.

'Hold on' he cried as the ship lunged out of the sand like a desert snake out of its hiding hole.

They blasted clear and were soon heading to outer space.

'I cannot believe we did not notice that there were two suits missing, the Martians had crafted two together to fit one of them.' said Professor James.

'That is not what concerns me.' said Giles. 'I am sure I heard the creature shout wait.'

'That has me stumped as well.' said Professor James.

'Maybe they just learnt their first word.' said Penny looking in her note book.

'Well it was too late to beg for mercy you do not sneak up on someone. What did it expect?'

'I agree. It was you or him.' said Giles.

Penny scratched her head but remained silent.

'We must warn Queen Victoria and the British Government as soon as we return.' said Gilbert.

'Quite.' said Professor James.

They did not need any gas from the plants to fall asleep and they all feasted as now they were back in the ship there was plenty, they ate and drank and smoked. Soon their eyelids became burdensome and they all fell asleep.

Unbeknownst to them the plants did release their soporific gaseous excrement sending them into an ever deeper sleep.

'Wake up, wake up.' cried Penny shaking her uncle violently, Professor James dreamed he was on Mars being questioned by a Martian when it suddenly grabbed him by the shoulders he awoke with a jolt and clenched his fist but was pleased to see it was Penny. He instantly registered the stress on her face.

'What is it?'

'The plants are dying; all of them.' cried Penny.

'They can't be.' said he.

'They are. Look.' replied she holding one up in her hand, it had shrunk and was turning a brown orange colour.

Professor James looked up at the ceiling and saw all the leaves turning brown.

'That's how they looked when they put us to sleep.'

'No, they were orange and brown.' said Gilbert.

'Oh you're awake.'

'So am I.' said Giles and I am afraid he is right they are brown and are starting to whither.

'Let us not panic for a minute. Where are we?' said Professor James.

'Steer the ship round like you did previously.' said Giles.

'Ok, I am going to turn us, everyone keep your eye out for anything familiar.' said Professor James wrestling with the controls. They had barely begun to turn when a planet came into view.'

'I see something familiar.' cried Penny.

'Confound it. It's Earth.' said Gilbert standing up.

Professor James looked up and stared at Giles with incredulity.

They approached the Earth's atmosphere and the ship started heating up as they entered it.

'It was not like this on the way up. The ship is falling apart I am telling you.' said Giles.

'Yes, something is not right.' said Professor James wiping a huge swathe of sweat from his forehead with his dust ridden shirt sleeve.

The craft started buffeting and rocking violently, a large green shard crossed the front of the screen like a bullet.

'Good God the armour is coming off now.' cried Giles.

'The controls are failing.' said Professor James and I can smell hot oil.

'The air is stifling, I am struggling to breathe.' said Gilbert.

'We all are,' cried Penny

'Just keep calm and breathe shallow, a few more minutes and we will be in the Earth's atmosphere.'

They plummeted like coconuts heading for someone's head.

Professor James wrestled with the controls with all his might, sweat was running down his palms and into every crevice, dripping off his eyebrows into his eyes but he could not let go despite the stinging. Professor James knew the reason they were so hot was because their armour was failing. How was this possible?

Finally they saw blue sky.

'Hold on we are nearly there.' cried Professor James.

'Let us open the door get some air.' said Gilbert.

'Are you mad? We are still way too high up, we will be sucked out and cannot breathe the air.'

'Another chunk of armour just came off.' said Giles

'I know I felt the ship move. We need to fall as far as we can then open the chutes, as soon as we do we can kick the door open but hold onto something as the air pressure will probably create a vacuum.'

'Where on the Earth are we coming down?' said Gilbert.

'Not sure, it looked like the Indian ocean.' said Giles.

The Earth got closer and rather than looking like a curious inviting object it now appeared as a solid menace that they were about to slam into.

'Get ready,' shouted Professor James.

'Look there is a ship, do you think you can steer us toward it, if they see us come down then we should be rescued.'

'Excellent idea Giles.' said Penny clapping her hands.

'Everyone get ready to jump out as this will sink like a stone from a quarry.' said Giles.

Giles looked at Professor James.

'We have to get out immediately James, all of us, I am warning you I have seen how fast mighty ships can sink and they are built to float, this is not.'

'Penny as soon as we stop you undo your harness and make straight for the door.' said Professor James.

Professor James grappled with the controls and hit the booster, the craft shifted violently. 'It worked.' cried he.

'Ready?' said Giles.

'Now.' cried Professor James.

Giles yanked the lever, the parachutes were deployed and they felt themselves jerked forward as the parachutes took hold. The looked and saw green rain falling from them.

'The armour is disintegrating and falling.'

'Do not worry Giles we have plenty left back at Ians' said Gilbert.

'No we do not.'

'What do you mean we do not?' said Professor James.

'We took it all with us.' replied he.

'Do not ridicule me man.'

'No, Professor James we did.' said Penny I nearly commented earlier but thought I had better not.

'What kind of confounded lunatic would not leave any behind?'

'I do not think we paid attention. It was only on the way up here that I had the thought that we had not actually left any behind and if the test flight failed then it could have all been over even if we did survive.'

'Never mind for now, we are alive, let us be grateful for that.'

'Perhaps you are right in that Penny.' said Gilbert.

'Everybody hold on, I am kicking open the door, I can hardly breathe.' said Giles.

Giles kicked the door, it opened straight away, a lot easier than it should have.

'We are getting close now I can see the ship in detail.' said Professor James.

'Look the people on deck are pointing at us.' squealed Penny. 'We are saved, she got up and threw her arms around her uncle's neck.'

XX A Book of Revelation

The craft swung in the wind as it descended and they hit the water with a large jolt, they all unbuckled themselves immediately as they had braced for impact. As the doors opened the warm Indian Ocean water flooded in and they all enjoyed getting wet after so much time without a wash. Professor James waited until Penny was out and then he was left aiding Gilbert. Giles was first out as he was right next to the door but did not shirk his duties and stayed to help everyone. The Mad Professor now only spattered with green rocks and full of dead plants sunk and took the parachutes with it.

The large wooden ship was right on top of them having manoeuvred to intercept. They climbed aboard, Professor James introduced himself. The Captain welcomed him warmly and said he was known only as Captain or the Captain. Professor James had his reservations he was polite enough with them as he had heard of Giles. To the crew on the ship however, he treated them with terrible contempt and abandonment, Professor James wondered how they had not mutinied yet. One night when the Captain was drunk he was a little too familiar toward Penny, Professor James could not contain himself and threw him up against the side of the ship and punched him in the stomach, then warned that he would tear his limbs off if he even looked at his niece for the rest of the trip, the Captain was the perfect host from that day forward.

They were indeed in the middle of the Indian Ocean and found out they were heading for Africa. They arrived in the port of Durban.

From Durban their trip was much more pleasant as they took first class. Professor James reached out to the university and dropped a line to Prince Albert for good measure. Doors magically swung open everywhere they went. They were rushed into the exquisite rooms in the most expensive hotels and booked in first class with their own cabin when at sea for the voyage home.

Once again they were to be at sea for many weeks when Penny grew emotional and stopped speaking to any one of them. Professor James knocked on her door and tried to reason with her but she would not listen and did not even want to speak to her darling uncle. All she kept on saying was that she knew it was not his fault and that she still loved him.

The situation filled Professor James full of angst as he was not used to worrying about someone like this considering he had no children of his own. He had already written to her father advising that she was safe and on her way home.

Gilbert, himself and Giles discussed it at length over whisky and cigars and deduced she must be referring to the deaths of Dennis and Ian. They all agreed that she would come around and just needed some time to grieve. In truth they all did but none of them showed it outwardly.

They were only a few days from England when Penny finally broke her silence.

She requested a private meeting and Professor James obtained a small room just for them complete with drinks, cigars and light food. Penny entered wearing a black dress to a sea of bewildered faces.

'As you know back on Mars I often said something was out of kilter.'

Professor James sucked heavily on a flaming pipe whilst Giles smoked a large cigar.

'I have been holding something back from you. When I entered the dead Martian room with my uncle, I spotted something laying on the floor, it was presumably in the Martians other hand when it was shot. It is a journal of some kind and written in some kind of code like alien language that I have set myself upon solving.'

'So that is why you had your head in that confounded notebook the whole time.' said Giles laughing.

'Yes but what I discovered is nothing to laugh about.'

'Do go on said Gilbert.' Taking a bite out of a ham and mustard sandwich.

'I have deciphered it well enough to understand what it is saying and we have made a total error of judgement.'

'In what way?' cried Professor James pointing his pipe at her.

'They were not trying to kill us or even harm us. They were trying to save us!'

'Save us By Jove, how?' said Giles forgetting to flick his cigar ash and idly letting a huge clump fall to the floor.

'I am still trying to work out their numerical system but it turns out that sometime in the future the Earth will run out of oxygen and that is why they sent that meteorite, the plant has an affinity with it and will grow happily on it even in the harshest of conditions.'

'Such as deep space.' said Gilbert.

'Quite.' said Professor James relighting his pipe.

'You see all those rocks we saw had tiny buds in to populate the Earth so we would not die, oxygen would be abundant and even better than before. They were not sure how much of the meteorite would burn up hence they only used a small sample to begin with and placed it in a really protected place'

'What were the ships for?' asked Professor James.

'In case the plan failed; they planned to rescue us. Don't you see that is why they let us be, they were trying to help us, when they held up their hand they were pleading with us to stop until we killed so many of them that they had no choice to surrender on the meadow. We destroyed a whole city, we got it all wrong, it is so terrible I have been struggling to process it, I feel like I just want to live in a cave somewhere away for all existence.'

'What about the injection?' asked Professor James.

A solitary tear slid down Penny's face like condensation down a window.

'It was supposed to help us cope with minimal oxygen, they had worked for years to develop it and even had an antidote in case it was harmful to us. I agree it was too risky but they had dedicated themselves to saving our lives'

'Confound it!' said Professor James putting his head into his hand.

Penny looked at Giles and Gilbert who both looked to be in a state of mumchance.

'They're biggest frustration was that they could not understand us, they had studied our planet and attempted to understand our body language. I found a note about one Martian who was convinced that he could learn to speak human and had become obsessed by it, I am guessing that is who we met at the Mad Professor.'

'The one I killed you mean?'

'Yes Uncle. I'm afraid so.'

The room fell silent. Professor James and Giles sucked their tobacco desperately as if they might find their salvation within it. Gilbert looked despondent and got one of Professor James's cigarettes and lit it, drawing on it heavily. Professor James's eyes moistened but he never shed a tear.

Three weeks later Professor James was sitting by his fire in his red leather arm chair, smoking his pipe and looking into the flames, watching haunted faces torture him and demand him for answers. He pondered the Martian and with his new knowledge he felt his bowels tighten when he thought of the first Martian that he had killed, it was trying to save Penny's life and he murdered it in cold blood. He saw the face of his old friend Ian idly chatting to him asking why he left him on Mars. He saw the smile as he fell, every time he closed his eyes and when he opened them. Professor James glanced to the table next to him and saw the half empty bottle of whisky on the table, he looked back at the fire and saw Dennis young and alive wondering what had happened to him. Was it right for anyone to die on Mars?

In a spate of defiance he poured himself another large glass and relit his pipe, he reran the expedition and thought of all the innocent lives they had needlessly slain. He thought of the cave-ins and realised he had murdered a civilisation over a misunderstanding. Professor James held up his glass of whisky to the flames, the refraction through the glass made the fire seem alive and omnipotent with an ever-alluring magical quality. As he was drawn into the mirage of fire dance he remembered the cruel irony that the Martians were trying to save them.

'Perhaps it was best they didn't.' said he.

THE FIRST MAN TO MARS

If you enjoyed The First Man to Mars, please consider adding an Amazon review. You can find the Amazon page by clicking the link.

www.amazon.com/dp/B089Q1K313

I would be very grateful if you could spare five minutes to do that. It need only be a line or two and it does make a massive difference.

All the best,

Jon-Jon

Afterword

How about a **FREE BOOK?**

One of the most enjoyable things about being a writer is building relationships with my readers. I send out newsletters with updates about my writing journey, new releases, news and other exciting titbits.

Simply join my mailing list to collect your **FREE** copy of **VICTORIAN ADVENTURE STORIES** plus a bonus short story (exclusive to my mailing list) by signing up at:

www.jon-jon.co.uk

VICTORIAN ADVENTURE STORIES
ELEVEN TALES SET IN THE REIGN OF QUEEN VICTORIA

A reputed and feared gangster meets the love of his life and attempts to get out of a gang. But betrayal to the Dreaded Doctor will lead to fatal consequences. Can this henchman protect himself, his new love and find a way out alive?

Do you like tales of mystery, intrigue and adventure? If so you will love Victorian Adventure Stories. Eleven tales all set in the reign of Queen Victoria during the 19th Century. Written in Jon-Jon's own 'Adventure Classic' style and salted with killer twists, you can expect Dinosaurs, Ghosts, Strange Creatures, Villains, Disasters, Gamblers, Romance and much more!

Other Titles by Jon-Jon

Tiger! Tiger! Tiger!

My Debut Adventure Novel Out Now!

'Fantastic Read!'
'Killer Twist!'
'Characters are Great!'
'Fully Recommend this Book!'

In an unforgiving jungle the question of Man vs Beast is about to be answered once and for all ...

Colonial India, a land that attracts hunters such as Charles, a man obsessed with killing the tiger that had long evaded him. With a team of friends and a skilled shikari he pursues his striped tormentor. But the King of Cats is no easy foe. As the jungle dances with war and worlds collide will the King of the Cats triumph or will man have his way?

AVAILABLE NOW!

http://www.amazon.com/dp/B0722N94L9

The Jellyset Kid

Meet Warwick, a young boy who after drinking unset Jelly awakes to discover it has set *into* his body giving him superhero like abilities. Struggling to keep his powers a secret whilst trying to win the heart of Faustine, he begins to battle the bad guys but is he the only one out there with superpowers?

The Jellyset Kid will be released Saturday 18th July 2020!

Learn more at

www.Jon-Jon.co.uk

Aaron the Alien

Meet Timmy; an ordinary young boy who is shocked not only to meet an Alien but to meet one as mouthy as he is.

After arguing about whose planet is the best they set off to visit Aaron's and end up crashing en route. Timmy and Aaron quickly realise that they are stranded on Bejjerwejjertejnej, a world as terrifying as it is comical.

Will they find a way off the planet? Can they stay alive long enough to do so? Do they really know each other?

Release Date Coming Soon on Aaron's Website!

www.aaronthealien.com

About the Author

Jon-Jon was born Jon Jones in the South Midlands, UK and now lives in central London where he writes Victorian Adventure, YA, Children's & Travel.

For more information please visit:

www.Jon-Jon.co.uk

For his Aaron the Alien series visit:

www.AarontheAlien.com

Or you can contact Jon-Jon via

JonJonWriting@yahoo.co.uk

twitter.com/JonJonWrites

fb.me/JonJonWrites

Facebook.com/tigernovel

Printed in Poland
by Amazon Fulfillment
Poland Sp. z o.o., Wrocław